The Reverse of the Curse Series, Book 3

Vampires 201

R. Stone

The Reverse of the Curse Series (c) Copyright 2014
Vampires 201 by R. Stone

Cover Artist: Tatiana Vila
Formatted by: Jesse Gordon
Publisher: The Mad Writer
Editor: Shelly Stone
ISBN-13: 978-0615981277
ISBN-10: 0615981275

Pre-requisite is "Vampires 101 and 200."
Vampires 202, "The Immortals," coming soon.

CHAPTER 1
LUKE AND CALICIA

I stood in the great room of the log cabin that I once called home and faced Calicia Claig.

She smiled at me. "Is she awake yet Lukas?"

I looked directly into her ice cold blue eyes. "Don't call me Lukas you know that I hate it and no, she is still unconscious. Now let's talk about my money you have Ariel and I want my million dollars."

"All in good time Lukas. So tell me, did you have to travel far to get to Canada?"

I laughed at her. "Good try Calicia, you don't need to know where I have been living. Give me my money."

A wicked smile spread across her face. "What's the hurry Lukas?"

I took a step toward her. "I have plans of my own Calicia the money, now!"

She didn't flinch. "Are you sure that you won't re-consider and rejoin our coven? After all, this is your home."

"No, Calicia it was my home when my father was alive and besides you have built up quite an army of vam-pires, I don't recognize anyone. How many are in your coven now?"

"Oh about thirty or so, but still Lukas this is where you belong."

"I want the money Calicia now!"

Calicia smiled at me again, "Oh, alright! You were al-ways such a troublesome boy, follow me."

I walked behind Calicia and followed her out of the great room and down the long hallway that led to my father's den. The minute I walked in the den memories of him flooded my mind - his scent still lingered.

Calicia looked over at me. "Yes Lukas, I can still smell his cologne in here too."

"Just get to it Calicia." I watched as she turned away from me and approached the bookcase that sat behind my father's desk. She reached underneath one of the book shelves and instantly it slid sideways into the wall, revealing a cast iron safe.

"If you don't mind Lukas, just wait over there by the door while I get your money."

"When did you have that put in?"

She laughed. "It was years ago dear boy."

I walked over and stood by the door. "Just hurry up Calicia, I plan on leaving as soon as I get my money." I could hear the dial turning on the safe and I listened at each click as she turned it in the hopes of memorizing the combination.

Calicia opened the safe, reached into it, closed it and then turned back around to face me. "Here you go Lukas, one-hundred-thousand dollars."

She held a stack of cash in her hand and I could easily tell that it was not a million dollars. "I knew that I couldn't trust you, the deal was for a million."

"And you will get it just as soon as I get what I want, the two doctors. You didn't think that I would just hand you a million dollars for that little red-headed shrimp did you? How do I even know that you really know the two vampire doctors that I seek?"

I raised my voice at her. "One phone call Calicia and they will come to her rescue but I won't make it for only a hundred-thousand dollars, so you had better dig a little deeper into that safe of yours." I could tell by the look on her face that she hadn't expected this from me the corners of her mouth cringed slightly. It was a look I recognized, she was angry. I watched while she sat the stack of cash down on the desk and then moved back to the safe, opened it again, hastily reached into it and removed several more stacks of cash and turned and sat them on the desk. With one hand she reached out and slammed the safe door shut.

Calicia turned to face me. "Ok, Luke, three-hundred thousand dollars, that's all until I see the doctors. After that you will get the rest of your money, vampires honor."

I shook my head at her. "You have no honor Calicia."

Calicia smiled. "Spoken like a true southern gentleman Lukas. I swear sometimes you remind me of your father. Take the three-hundred thousand or leave it?"

I nodded my head at her. "Ok, Calicia agreed, three-hundred thousand now and the rest when they arrive, but I am warning you, if you cross me you will be sorry." I could tell by her smile that my threat had meant nothing to her, she looked amused. I quickly scooped up the piles of cash from the desktop and put them into the backpack that I had brought. I followed her out of the room and she locked the door and then turned back around to me. "Don't forget to check on our little guest, she will probably be confused about her new surroundings once she awakes."

CHAPTER 2
THE PLAN

I sat at the desk in my medical clinic on the third floor of our home. It had been twenty-four hours since Luke had taken Ariel and I was worried sick. I had expected a phone call from Luke, but it hadn't come yet. My cell phone rang and I instantly picked it up and hit talk, "Hello."

"Hello, Alexander, it is Charles. Have you heard anything from Luke yet?"

"No Charles not yet, how about you, did you learn anything that could help us?"

"Yes, I contacted a few of my old friends but I am afraid that the news is not very good. It seems that Luke's real name is Lukas Edmond Lee and he used to belong to Calicia Claig's coven in Canada. The coven was originally started by Luke's father Earl O. Lee about a hundred and fifty years ago. They were from the South, but moved to Canada when he married Calicia Claig.

Earl met with an untimely death shortly after his marriage to Calicia and she took over his coven and Luke left shortly after that. I am afraid that Calicia has the reputation of being quite "Ruthless" within the vampire community."

"Do you know where her coven is located?"

Charles sighed. "No I am afraid not, but I am working on that."

"What are your thoughts Charles, do you think that Luke is after money?"

"Perhaps, but I think it might be something more than that Alexander, did Luke know anything about the work that you and Antoinette are doing?"

"No, I don't think so, wait a moment Charles! I just remembered something, the fight we had at the school with Luke and his friends, when we anesthetized Matt, Luke may have guessed what happened. Our neighbor Mrs. Crabitz also told Antoinette that she saw someone snooping around our house. If Luke was in our house and saw the medical equipment he could have put two and two together".

"That could be Alexander, but surely he couldn't have guessed what the equipment was for? I do believe however, that based on what you've told me about him that he has a high intellect."

"I appreciate the analysis Charles and I agree he is very smart. But what worries me even more is that he seems to have a personal interest in Ariel."

"Oh, Alexander I am sorry to hear that."

I sighed. "Yes, Charles I fear the worst, that he has changed her."

"Yes, that is a strong possibility but you can always change her back."

"I know, but she would never be the same. If she were changed and then harmed someone, as a vampire I mean, I don't think that she could forgive herself. This is my fault I knew the risks of falling in love with a human."

"Alexander calm down, we don't know if she has been changed. Try and stay positive."

"I know, but there was so much blood on her apartment wall. I am worried that she is either dead or has been changed."

"Well, it only happened last night so if she were changed she would still be unconscious. There is still time for you to intervene. I expect that he will be contacting you at any time with his demands."

I sighed. "I hope you are right Charles."

"Everything will be alright Alexander. I am still making inquiries to try and find out where her coven is located. I will be in contact with you soon."

"Thank you very much Charles, please call as soon as you learn something, goodbye."

"Goodbye."

I hung the phone up and sensed Antoinette's presence. I turned slightly in my chair. "Hello sister."

"Alexander, was that Charles?"

"Yes it was."

"Was he able to get any information for us?"

"Yes, he told me that Luke's real name is Lukas Earl Lee and that he belonged to a coven in Canada. It was originally his father's coven, but his father is dead and it now belongs to his step mother Calicia Claig. Charles said that Luke left the coven some time ago."

"I thought as much."

Alexander nodded his head at me. "Yes, you were right Antoinette he has been trying to start his own coven here in Portland."

"Does Charles know where the coven is located?"

"No, he is trying to find out. He did say however, that Calicia does not have a good reputation within the vampire community."

"What do you think Luke wants from us?"

"It must be the anesthesia. When I was talking to Charles I remembered that Mrs. Crabitz had told us that she had seen someone enter our house, remember?"

"Yes."

"Well Luke might have put two and two together, meaning that if he saw the medical equipment in our home, he might have suspected that Matt had been anesthetized."

"I hope you are right Alexander and that he has only guessed about the anesthesia and has not learned our secret."

"How could he Antoinette?"

I didn't answer my brother right away. I knew that my answer would upset him, but the look on his face told me that he had guessed what I was about to say, "Maybe Ariel told him?"

Alexander stood from his chair and looked at me. "You can't be serious Antoinette? She would never do that."

I looked directly into his eyes. "How can you be so sure Alexander? Can you imagine how scared she might be? Could you blame her if she did?" I had upset him.

"Stop it, just stop it Antoinette."

"Look, I am sorry I know that I am upsetting you but you have to face reality. We knew this would be dangerous, dangerous to Ariel and dangerous to us and our work."

Alexander narrowed his eyes at me. "You resent her, don't you?"

I remained silent.

"You do Antoinette, you really do?"

I didn't want to upset Alexander any more than I already had but he needed to face reality. "Alexander she has put our life's work in jeopardy. If we do rescue her and if she is unharmed you are going to have to change her! It is the only way that she will be safe in the future while we continue our work."

Alexander sat back down in his chair. "You can't be serious? That is not a solution that would be a disaster."

"A disaster may have already occurred Alexander, they might already know about the reversal process."

Alexander tilted his head downward. "This is what I feared Antoinette that other vampire covens would intervene but I didn't expect it to happen this soon. I guess it really doesn't matter anyway".

"What do you mean?"

"Well, if they know about the anesthesia they will start to wonder what it is for and eventually guess what we are doing."

"Oh, Alexander I didn't think about that."

Alexander picked up his cell phone. "Why hasn't he called yet? What if he really doesn't want anything from us and the message on the wall in her apartment was just a distraction? Maybe Luke just wanted to turn her for himself?"

I could see the anguish in my brother's face, he was suffering terribly. "Please Alexander try not to think about that, we need to stay focused in order to rescue her."

"You are right sister, what would I do without you? You always know just the right thing to say to me. Are Zack and Jeremy here yet?"

"No they are on the way they were in downtown Portland when I called them. When they arrive they will help Mia and I pack the Hummer. I am going to pack some medical supplies in case we need them for Ariel."

"Do you want me to help?"

I put my hand on my brother's shoulder. "No, we've got it. You need to stay by the phone in case Luke or Charles calls. We will take care of everything else." I withdrew my hand.

"Antoinette, what are we going to do about our class? We have two days left in this semester."

I smiled at Alexander. "I already took care of that. I called Principle Hines and told him that Ariel had a family emergency and that I would be covering her class for the next two days. He was ecstatic about the idea of me teaching her class."

Alexander looked at me inquisitively. "Yes, but you won't be there to teach her class or ours?"

I nodded my head at him. "Yes, but I have another idea. I am going to call Mirka and ask if she, Lauren and Joseph would act as teacher's aids for us. I have her cell phone number on our class roster. They are our best students and seem to really take an interest during class. I am sure that they would love to volunteer to substitute teach for the last two days of class for extra credit. Between the three of them they can handle Ariel's class and our class for just two hours a day for two days."

"What about Principle Hines?"

"He doesn't need to know that we are gone."

Alexander persisted. "Yes but what if he comes to class, or needs something from us?"

I laughed. "Let's not sweat the small stuff right now ok? I am sure Mirka, Lauren and Joseph can fend him off for a couple of days. Trust me, it will work."

"It's not a bad idea and I guess we really have no other choice. Thanks Antoinette for being so supportive, I mean, I know that you are not really that found of Ariel."

"Alexander it's not that I dislike her or anything, actually she was starting to grow on me, just a little but I am worried about our work." I sensed Mia's presence and turned to look at her. "Hello Mia."

Mia walked in the room and stood next to me. "Hi Antoinette, any word yet?"

"No Mia. Let's go back downstairs and leave Alexander alone."

"Sure Antoinette."

Mia followed me out of Alexander's office and down to the second floor and into my office. "I need to call one of our students, Mirka." I stopped at my desk.

Mia stood next to me. "Wow Antoinette, this room is awesome I have never been in here before. It is almost as nice as your bedroom. Look at those mahogany book cases they go all the way to the ceiling, they are absolutely gorgeous."

"Yes, I love them. I had them shipped all the way from England. They were actually in our parent's house."

"These books are so old."

I smiled at her. "Yes, I collect old books."

Mia's eyes swept the room. "And I love the purple corded drapery. Is this a Monet painting?"

"Yes."

"Is it a real Monet?"

"Yes."

"Awesome, I love how you decorate. My room is the only room in the house that is different. I really like the modern art deco stuff, I hope you don't mind?"

I shook my head sideways at her. "Absolutely not Mia, I told you that you could decorate it however you wished and I think it looks lovely. I am just going to make this call real quick." I found Mirka's cell phone number on the class roster and dialed it, it rang and she answered. "Hello Mirka, this is Antoinette Von-Allenberg."

"Hello Ms. Von-Allenberg."

"I was hoping that you, Joseph and Lauren could do a favor for Alexander and me?"

"Sure, what's up?"

"Well, Ms. Domande was called away on a family emergency and I was going to cover her class for the last two days of the semester but now Alexander and I have a family emergency as well. I was wondering if you three would like to play teacher's aid for both classes for two hours a day, the last two days of the semester."

Mirka sounded enthused. "Are you serious? That would be awesome!"

"We would give you extra credit for substitute teaching."

"Great, but what do we do during class?"

I laughed. "No worries, I have an outline for both classes for you to follow. I will fax it to the office and it will be in my mailbox in the teacher's lounge. Oh! And when you take attendance go ahead and mark Mia as present, she is with Alexander and I."

"Sure thing I can't wait. I will call Joseph and Lauren tonight and let them know about it."

"That sounds like a good idea. Mirka, there is just one more thing and it is really important."

"Sure, what is it?"

"Well, Principle Hines knows that Ariel is out for the next few days on a family emergency, but he doesn't know that Alexander and I have been called away, so it's sort of a secret."

"Ok, but what does that mean exactly?"

"Well, it really shouldn't be a problem, I mean he has never come to our classroom while we were teaching but, in the event that he does, just simply tell him that Alexander stepped away for a moment and if he comes to Ariel's class where I am supposed to be teaching tell him the same thing. Do you think that you could do that for us?"

Mirka laughed. "No problem, I think I understand."

"Mirka, this really means a lot to us, thank you very much and if you need me for anything, save my cell number in your phone."

"Ok Ms. Von-Allenberg, I will see you when you get back. We all signed up for your class next semester, "The Immortals," what is it about exactly?"

"We will be discussing the Egyptians and some other ancient cultures that drank blood and sought immortality."

Mirka's voice was a high pitched shrill. "Oh, I can't wait. We are really enjoying the classes."

"Thank you Mirka, see you when we get back."

"Good bye, Ms. Von-Allenberg."

I hung up the phone and turned to Mia. "Well that worked out well. Come on Mia let's go downstairs and wait for Zack and Jeremy."

Mia followed me out of the room and down the staircase. I slid down the banister of the last set of stairs as usual and landed in the foyer and then straightened up my body. "Let's go outside and wait for them, they should be here any minute?"

"Ok, Antoinette."

We walked out of the house and onto the front porch and sat down on the top step of stairs, Mia sat next to me.

Mia looked over at me. "Antoinette, I hope Ariel is ok?"

"Me too, I have never seen Alexander like this, he is so angry. I am afraid of what he might do if something has happened to her."

Mia looked curious. "What do you mean?"

I shook my head at her. "Never mind, let's just try and think positive. I have a feeling that Ariel is still alive, but I am worried that Luke might have changed her."

Mia laughed. "Well if he has, you and Alexander can change her back?"

"Yes, but Alexander is worried. If Luke did change her and she kills a human to feed, he doesn't think that she would ever be able to forgive herself, I mean because she is so religious."

"Oh, I hadn't thought about that. It is difficult I know that first hand, Tara, Dorian and I all had to fight the urge and the thirst to turn away from humans, it was so hard and there were times when I didn't think I could do it."

"Yes, but you did do it and it helped because, you had each other. Ariel is alone with Luke and the others, you know how he is?"

Mia put her head down. "Yes, I do."

"Mia, while we wait for Jeremy and Zack we could practice using your gift, you are getting much better at controlling it or we could go in the backyard and go over some fighting techniques."

Mia turned her head away from me, "Antoinette who is that?"

"Who are you talking about?"

"Over there, that woman peeking out of the windows of that house."

I turned my head toward Mr. and Mrs. Crabitz's house and then laughed. "That is our nosey next door neighbor Mrs. Crabitz."

"Oh that's the neighbor you were talking about."

I nodded my head at her. "Yes, that woman will not leave us alone. She saw Zack and Jeremy on the roof a couple of times and we haven't heard the end of it."

"You weren't kidding, she really is a nuisance."

I stood up. "Come on Mia, let's get off the steps and go over and stand by my rose bushes where she can't see us." I walked down the steps and out onto the lawn and over to the roses.

Mia followed me. "These are really gorgeous Antoinette, you have a green thumb."

I smiled at her. "I love gardens and flowers. We gardened a lot in England." Just then I sensed Zack and

Jeremy's presence. "Zack and Jeremy are here." I turned my head as they approached the house and watched as they stopped near the wrought iron gate that led into our yard but before I could yell out to them they jumped over the gate in one leap. "Oh no Mia, I hope Mrs. Crabitz didn't just see them jump that five foot gate." I moved toward them. "Hey guys, watch the leaping over the gate thing, the nosey neighbor is already peaking out of her window at us."

Zack laughed. "Oops, I am sorry Antoinette."

Just then Mrs. Crabitz came running out of her front door and down her steps toward the wrought iron fence that separated our yards. "Ah, ha I knew it! You are the two boys that I saw on the roof. I knew that Antoinette knew you."

I momentarily looked at Mia, Zack and Jeremy and then walked to the fence line where Mrs. Crabitz stood. "I am sorry, what did you say Mrs. Crabitz?"

She ranted on. "I told Albert, I told him that you knew the boys that I saw on the roof."

Zack, Jeremy and Mia had walked over and stood at my side.

Mrs. Crabitz shook her fist in the air and then pointed at Zack and Jeremy. "I saw you two boys on that rooftop several times."

She was making a scene and yelling a little too loudly. There was another neighbor out in his yard just a couple of houses down the street and out of the corner of my eye I saw that he turned his head toward us for a moment but then walked in his house. "Please Mrs. Crabitz, just calm down I am sure there is a logical explanation for everything."

The corners of Mrs. Crabitz mouth cringed upward. "Oh, you are a smooth one, Antoinette. So calm all the time, trying to make Albert think that I am crazy."

I laughed at her. "I don't think that you need me for that Mrs. Crabitz."

Mrs. Crabitz yelled louder. "How dare you say such a thing? Albert, Albert, come out here!"

I didn't know what to do and then all of a sudden Mrs. Crabitz just slowly collapsed to the ground and lay underneath the shade of her lemon tree where she had been standing. I looked over at Mia. "Did you just do that?"

Mia smiled at me. "Yes, sorry, I couldn't take her voice any longer."

I laughed. "Thanks."

Jeremy stepped closer to the fence line. "Shouldn't we do something?"

I smiled at him. "Like what wake her up? I don't think so. She will be fine in a while, there is a nice cool breeze out and she is in the shade."

Zack laughed and looked at Mia. "That's an awesome gift Mia it works like magic."

I looked at them. "Come on you guys it is getting late we need to get the Hummer packed, as soon as Charles calls Alexander we need to hit the road." Just as we walked into the garage I saw Mr. Crabitz walking out of his front door. I closed the garage door.

* * *

"Wanda, Wanda where are you? Wanda what are you doing under that tree. Are you alright?"

"Stop shaking me Albert. What happened why am I lying under the lemon tree?"

"I don't know. Here let me help you up. I heard you calling for me and I walked out of the house and saw you lying under the tree, you must have passed out. Do you feel alright?"

"Yes, I feel fine, actually I feel quite refreshed."

"Wanda what happened?"

"I don't know one minute I was talking with Antoinette and her friends, a young girl and those two boys that I had seen on the roof and that's the last thing I remember!"

"Oh, don't start that again Wanda, remember what Dr. Martin told you, maybe you need to take another one of your pills?"

"Albert, you are being ridiculous I only went to see Dr. Martin because you insisted. I know what I saw before and I know what I saw today. Those two boys just arrived at Antoinette's house and they jumped over the front gate in a single leap."

"So?"

"So, Albert it is that gate over there, the main gate to the yard."

"That's ridiculous Wanda that gate is five or six feet high no one could just jump over it, not even with a running start."

"They did, both of them. They walked right up to it and then just jumped up in the air and went right over it."

"You are seeing things again Wanda, it is back to Dr. Martin for you."

CHAPTER 3
ON THE ROAD

I watched as Alexander ran through the garage door and over to the Hummer holding his cell phone. "Let's go Antoinette! Luke is on the phone with me now."

I looked over at Zack, Jeremy and Mia we had just finished packing the Hummer. "Ok Alexander we are ready, everyone get in." I could hear Luke's voice on the other end of Alexander's phone.

Alexander yelled into the phone at Luke. "Now tell me where she is?"

I got in the drivers seat and Alexander climbed in the passenger seat and Mia, Zack and Jeremy got in the rear passenger seat. I started the Hummer up and backed it out of the garage and began driving. I listened as Luke spoke to Alexander - "Patience Alexander patience, listen to me carefully so that you get the directions right I wouldn't want you ending up at the wrong place. Time is of the essence."

Alexander responded and sounded furious. "You had better not touch one hair on her head Luke or so help me I will rip you and your friends to shreds."

I could hear Luke laughing and then he continued to talk to Alexander – "You must have been so worried that I wouldn't call and I bet you are worried that I changed her too, I guess you won't know until you get here. I must admit though I see what you find so very attractive about her."

I saw the hairs stand up on Alexander's neck. "I swear Luke, if you hurt her I will…"

Luke's voice rang out from Alexander's cell phone – "Just listen, you and Antoinette will be traveling alone to Canada and bring that medicine that you have, that makes vampire's sleep, whatever it was that you gave to Matt and Darla. If you leave now you should be here by dawn. Once you get into Canada stay on the highway and pass through Quebec. You will travel until you see the "Setinee" exit, take it and bear to the right. Are you getting all of this?"

"Yes, get on with it!"

Luke continued giving Alexander directions. "Bear to the right until you come to County Road 234, then turn right and follow that road up the base of the mountains. Drive until the road ends you will see a big log garage. The garage sits at the base of a small mountain full of jutting sharp rocks and boulders. Leave your vehicle at the garage. You will have to make the rest of the trip on foot up the mountain to the cabin. There are no trails so you will have to climb straight up. The cabin is not accessible to humans unless they are expert rock climbers or have a helicopter. "Are you listening to me?"

"Yes, Luke I've got it. We are on the way."

Luke laughed. "And don't try – anything funny Alexander, Calicia is not as forgiving as I am."

"I am warning you Luke……. Hello, Hello!"

Alexander threw his cell into his lap and turned his head toward me. "He hung up on me. We should have left last night or early this morning and just started driving toward Canada, it is almost noon now and it has been over thirty hours since he took her. He wouldn't tell me if he changed her, if he did the change would be about complete now."

I was driving as fast as I could and heading for the interstate while Mia, Jeremy and Zack sat silently in the back seat. I turned my heard toward my brother. "Alexander, did he give you any indication as to whether or not she was ok?"

Alexander shook his head. "Not really, he just said to hurry."

"What does he want?"

"The anesthesia, as you suspected sister."

I watched while Alexander opened up the glove box and took out a pen and notepad. He started writing and I assumed he was writing the directions that Luke had given him.

Just then Alexander's phone rang and he grabbed it with warp speed. "Hello?"

I could hear Charles voice on the other end of the phone. "Hello Alexander I have some more information for you."

"Charles, I just heard from Luke. We are on our way to Canada. Luke gave me directions to a cabin where he has Ariel at".

Charles sighed. "Great Alexander I am so glad."

"I hope that she is alright Charles, I don't trust him."

"The reason I called was to tell you that I had obtained a general location of where Calicia Claig's coven is - but now you have the exact directions."

"Yes, thank you so much Charles for all that you have done. I know that you put yourself and your family at risk, I mean contacting your old coven and some of your friends."

"Don't give it a second thought Alexander, everything here is fine. You let me know if we can do anything else for you."

"I will."

Charles's voice took on a serious tone. "And please be careful Alexander. What I do know about Calicia Claig is that she has no regard for human or vampire life. She doesn't take prisoners and I am afraid that you will have to play dirty with her, you know what I mean?"

"Yes Charles, I understand. We will be careful." I hung up the phone. I knew that Charles meant that we would more than likely have to destroy some vampires, a thought that I didn't relish. We rode in silence for quite some time.

Zack – tapped my shoulder from the back seat. "Alexander, we should probably go over your plan so that we all know what you want us to do when we get there."

I turned my head sideways to him. "You are right Zack, I haven't told you guys what the plan is. Ok, here goes. Luke told me to leave the vehicle at a garage and said that we would have to climb a small mountain in order to reach the cabin. He said that the cabin is quite large, so I assume it must have at least three levels, maybe four. My first priority is to get Ariel out of the cabin as quickly as possible."

I turned my head to my brother as I drove. "Alexander just how are we supposed to get Ariel out of the cabin?" Somehow, I felt that I already knew the answer.

Alexander didn't smile. "It is simple Antoinette, first Zack, Jeremy and Mia will wait at the base of the mountain, near the Hummer and secondly you and I will go to the cabin as instructed and third, I will trade myself for Ariel."

I wanted to scream No! I wanted to object and argue with my brother, but I didn't dare to, not in front of everyone. This was Alexander's situation, it involved Ariel and I just couldn't get involved that way no matter how much it might hurt me to leave my brother in a house full of vampires. "Ok, then what?"

Alexander smiled. "I will tell this Calicia Claig that I will cooperate and give her whatever information she wants as long as she lets you and Ariel go."

"Then what happens?"

"Once you and Ariel reach the base of the cabin and get back to the Hummer I want Jeremy to take Ariel and leave in the Hummer. Then You, Mia and Zack will return for me with the injectors and we will finish this."

I knew what Alexander meant that we would be disposing of some vampires. I knew that this was hard for him to do, but it wouldn't be hard for me.

Alexander continued speaking. "When you, Zack and Mia return I want you to enter the cabin from the highest level and work your way down, take out as many vampires as you can. Each of you should carry at least six or seven injectors with you. Mia even though you can put some of the vampires to sleep with your gift, I still prefer that you carry a few injectors."

Mia nodded her head. "Ok Alexander."

Zack leaned up in his seat. "Alexander?"

"Yes Zack, what is it?"

"If you don't mind, I don't think I want to use the injectors, I mean I really have no need for them. I think I am better at just ripping off some heads."

"That's fine Zack whatever it takes. When you all reach the first floor of the cabin I will join you in the fight."

"Just out of curiosity though, how does the needle penetrate our skin, I mean our bodies are pretty resistant?" Zack asked.

"The needles are made out of titanium, my own invention."

"Cool," Zack said.

My brother's plan was daring. I momentarily closed my eyes and thought about the possibility that Alexander might not be alive by the time we got to the first floor of the cabin. "What if things go wrong…?"

Alexander shook his head at me. "Things won't go wrong Antoinette. Calicia is not going to dispose of me before I give her the formula for the anesthesia. She thinks that we are bringing the anesthesia to her, but once she learns that the formula is in my head that is my leverage to make her let you and Ariel go. She won't harm me until she gets what she wants."

Jeremy leaned forward in his seat. "Wow Alexander that sounds like a very organized plan."

"Thank you Jeremy, both Antoinette and I have had a lot of battle experience over the years."

"Yes, I suppose you do. Zack and I aren't quite as old or experienced but if you ever find yourself in a gun fight we would be the two to handle that. I am actually faster than Billy the Kid was with a pistol. I rode with him and I taught him how to shoot."

I interrupted my brother's conversation with Jeremy. "Jeremy, are you serious you taught him how to shoot? That's amazing!"

"Yes Antoinette and he got all the publicity, but he was a cool dude."

Zack started laughing. "Yes, that is an understatement he was a real party dude."

"Mia?"

"Yes, Antoinette?"

"I want you to use the injectors if you notice that you can't put the vampires out quickly enough on your own, ok?"

"Yes, I will use them if I need to."

Jeremy leaned up in his seat. "Alexander, exactly where do you want me to take Ariel once we rescue her."

"Head back to Portland. When we make it out of the cabin we will catch up with the Hummer."

Jeremy nodded his head in agreement. "Ok done."

"Ok, everyone we have a plan and it should work."

CHAPTER 4
BACK AT LINCOLN HIGH

I stood in Alexander's and Antoinette's classroom next to Joseph.

Joseph turned his head to me. "Are you nervous Mirka?"

I smiled at him. "No Joseph, this is so exciting, I can't wait to teach the class."

"Is Lauren in Mrs. Domande's classroom yet?"

I nodded my head at Joseph. "Yes, she will teach the Greek Mythology class this morning."

"What exactly did Antoinette say for us to do?"

"Relax Joseph. We just have to follow the outline that Antoinette faxed."

"Where is the outline?"

I pointed to the desk. "It is sitting on the desk and Lauren has the one for Greek Mythology."

"Did Antoinette tell you what the family emergency was?"

"No, she said that Ms. Domande had a family emergency and she and Alexander also had a family emergency but she didn't tell me what had happened. She said they would be gone today and tomorrow and that if Principle Hines stops by looking for them, we are to say that they just stepped out and will return shortly. Apparently he doesn't know that she and Alexander are gone."

Joseph's eyes widened. "Are you serious? We can't lie to Principle Hines."

I laughed. "Joseph, technically we are not lying, they did step out and will return in a few days."

Joseph sighed. "I guess that makes sense."

"Oh, there's the bell."

"Mirka, you can start off teaching if you want and I will just sit at the desk, let me know if you need help."

"Ok, Joseph, that's fine."

Joseph walked over and sat down at Alexander's desk.

The students walked in and took their seats and I stepped to the center of the room. I looked over at Joseph. "Joseph would you please close the classroom door it looks like everyone is here?"

"Ok Mirka." Joseph got up, walked over to the door, closed it and then returned to the desk and sat down.

I looked at the students. "Hello class, as you know I am Mirka and this is Joseph. Alexander and Antoinette are out today and tomorrow and asked Joseph and I to substitute teach in their absence."

I saw a hand go up and I couldn't remember the student's name. I thought it was kind of funny because I had been sitting in this class for the last seven weeks. I wondered how the teachers did it, I mean memorizing everyone's names. I called on him. "Yes, I am sorry I forgot your name?"

The student put his hand down. "I am Troy, where are Alexander and Antoinette at?"

"They got called away on a family emergency."

"Oh."

"Ok, if there are no more questions, let's get started. I need to take attendance." I looked around the room and a good part of the class was missing, Joseph and I were teaching, Lauren was in Ms. Domande's room, Melissa and Levi were dead and Luke, Darla, Matt, Jason, Tara and Dorian never returned to school and Mia was with Alexander and Antoinette. That only left six students. "Does anyone know where Luke and his friends are?"

Troy raised his hand again. "I heard that they got kicked out of school."

"Thank you, I hadn't heard that. Let's go around the room and everyone introduce your selves just to refresh my memory." I pointed to the first student.

"I am Troy," "Hope," "I am Karla," "Jake," "Amy," "I am Dan."

"Thanks. I have an outline that we need to follow so let's get started." I walked over to the desk and picked up a stack of papers and passed them out to the students. "This is an article that Antoinette wants you to read and then write your comments down about it. When you are finished please pass your papers forward. It is about an archeological dig that took place in Egypt several years ago, it's pretty interesting." I stepped back to the center of the room and stood for a moment while the students began reading the article and then I walked back to Antoinette's desk and sat down. "So far, so good," I thought to myself. I turned to Joseph, "Joseph why don't you run over and check on Lauren to see how she is doing?"

"Ok Mirka, I will be right back." Joseph stood up from his desk and walked out of the classroom. A few min-uets later he returned and walked over to me and bent over and whispered – into my ear. "Principle Hines stopped by Ms. Domande's classroom looking for Antoinette."

I looked up at him. "What happened?"

"Nothing, Lauren told him that Antoinette had to run back here for a few minuets."

"Terrific I hope he doesn't come here." Just then the classroom door opened and Principle Hines walked in and stood near the door. He looked confused when he saw me sitting at Antoinette's desk and Joseph standing next to me.

"Excuse me young lady, I am looking for Alexander or Antoinette?"

The entire classroom went silent. I stood from the desk to face him. "Oh, sorry Sir, they stepped out for a while. I am sort of watching class for her." I tried to be as subtle as I could.

Principle Hines didn't smile. "I see, well when either of them returns would you please let them know that I am looking for them?"

"Yes Sir, I will."

"Thank you." He turned and walked out of the door.

After Principle Hines left the classroom the entire class, all six students were staring at me. I stood up and moved to the center of the room and smiled at them. "It's complicated, sorry." They all laughed and then the bell rang. "Please pass your papers forward, thank you." They passed their papers forward and I collected them.

The students got up from their desks and walked out of the classroom.

Joseph walked over and stood next to me. "Mirka I am glad that you were here I don't think I could have handled that, you were so smooth."

I laughed. "Thanks Joseph, but I was a nervous wreck inside. We better get going or we will be late for our next class. I led the way to the door and switched off the classroom light and then opened the door. "Joseph, pull the door tight so that it locks."

"Ok Mirka." Joseph walked out after me and closed the door behind us.

* * *

I stood at my locker and David stood behind me.

"Hurry up Erin I want to get to the cafeteria while it is still lunch time."

"Chill out David, just let me put these books into my locker." I sat the books in the locker, closed the door and then put the combination lock back on and turned the dial. "There, I am done." I turned back around to face David and then we began walking to the cafeteria.

"Hey Erin, did you find anything else out about Luke and his friends?"

I shook my head at David. "No not yet, but I will. I know that they had something to do with Melissa and Levi's deaths."

David looked skeptical. "You can't be sure though?"

"Of course I am sure I just can't prove it. I called the police and talked with them yesterday."

David's eyes widened. "Dude, are you serious?"

I nodded my head at him. "Yes, they even came out to my house."

"And what happened?"

"They talked with me and my parents and I told them that I thought Luke and his friends had something to do with Melissa and Levi's deaths. I also told them that Darla had threatened Melissa that night at the dance."

"What did they say?"

"They said that I didn't have enough evidence and that just because Melissa told me that Darla threatened her at the dance that wasn't enough for them to do anything. I also told them that I saw Luke and his friends follow them out of the dance and that Melissa and Levi didn't have much to drink."

"What did they say about that?"

"They pretty much ignored what I said and told me that they shouldn't have been drinking at all. They also told me that they tried to contact Luke and his friends but couldn't find them. The names, addresses and telephone numbers that were on their school records were a fake."

David shook his head. "That is unreal I wonder who they really are?"

I shrugged my shoulders. "Wish I knew. I called some other high schools in Portland to see if they were registered and I can't find them so I am at a dead end right now. You got any ideas?"

"No, but I will think about it and see if I can come up with something, ok?"

"Ok, David thanks."

* * *

As I walked into the cafeteria I heard someone call my name. "Mirka." I looked around and saw Joseph and Lauren sitting at a table, Lauren waved at me and had saved a seat for me. I walked over to the table, pulled out a chair and sat down. "Hey you guys what's up?"

Lauren leaned toward me. "You are not going to believe what I heard?"

"What did you hear?"

Lauren sounded excited. "There is a rumor going around school that Melissa and Levi's death might not have been an accident."

"What do you mean, like murder?"

"I think so. Oh no! Don't look now but there is Erin and David."

I whipped my head around quickly to look at Erin and David as they walked into the cafeteria."

Lauren gently grabbed my arm. "Don't stare at them."

I turned my head back to her. "Why are you acting so weird Lauren?"

"Because they are the ones spreading the rumors, I also heard that they think that Luke and his friends had something to do with Melissa and Levi's deaths."

"Are you serious?"

She nodded her head at me. "Yes can you believe it? What if it is true? Don't you think that it is kind of weird, that Luke and his friends disappeared after Melissa and Levi died?"

"Yes, it is weird that they just vanished, but Mia is still here."

Lauren smiled. "Yes, and now she is friends with Alexander and Antoinette that is weird too?"

"I don't think that is weird".

Lauren persisted. "But Luke, Darla, Matt, Jason, Dorian and Tara are all gone, where did they go?"

Joseph entered the conversation. "Well, everyone is saying that they got kicked out of school."

Lauren shook her head at Joseph. "I don't buy it."

Joseph laughed. "Why don't you buy it Lauren?"

"Because Luke was nothing but trouble when he was here, he was a freak and it wouldn't surprise me if he did have something to do with their deaths. I don't think it's as simple as, he just changed schools."

Joseph laughed again. "So he was a freak, that doesn't mean that he is a murderer."

"No it doesn't but like I said, it wouldn't surprise me if he had something to do with what happened."

Just then Erin and David approached our table and stood next to it. "Hi, I am Erin and this is David."

I looked up at them. "I am Mirka and this is Lauren and Joseph."

Erin cleared his throat. "I don't know if you knew, but Melissa was my girlfriend and Levi was one of my best friends."

"Yes, I am very sorry, we all heard about the accident."

Erin shook his head. "Well, I don't think it was an accident. I know that you three were in that vampire class with Luke and his friends and I was wondering if you have seen them? I would like to talk to them."

"No sorry Erin we haven't seen them, not since the dance." I put my head down, I hadn't meant to remind him of that night at the dance when Melissa and Levi had died. "Sorry, I didn't mean…"

"No problem, it is ok."

Joseph looked up at Erin. "Why are you looking for Luke and his friends anyway?"

Erin stared at Joseph for a moment. "Because I think that he had something to do with Melissa and Levi's deaths, that's why."

"If we see them we will let you guys know," Joseph said.

Erin smiled at us. "Thanks."

David tugged on Erin's shirt sleeve. "Come on Erin let's go."

"Not yet, I am not through." Erin walked to the end of our table and stepped up on a chair and addressed the cafeteria loudly. "Excuse me everyone."

David tugged at Erin's shirt again. "Dude get down let's go."

Erin ignored David. "Can I have everyone's attention? Most of you know me I am Erin Lampbert, captain of our football team. I am sure that you all heard about Melissa and Levi's death last month, Melissa was my girl-friend. I would like to know if any of you have seen Luke and his friends. I am sure you all know who Luke is? The freak with the freaky friends, we all avoided last semester."

The entire cafeteria was at a dead silence.

Erin continued. "None of you have seen them?"

A voice called out from one side of the cafeteria, "No, not since the dance, why are you looking for him?"

Erin yelled back across the cafeteria. "The police want to talk to Luke and his friends and so do I, if anyone sees him let me know."

Several voices called out in response. "Yes," – "Sure dude," – "Will do."

"Thanks," Erin said and jumped down from the chair. David tugged at his sleeve once more. "Now can we go?"

"Yes."

Just then Principle Hines walked up to Erin. "What is going on here young man? I just caught the tail end of your speech."

Erin looked up at Principle Hines. "Nothing Sir, I was just looking for a couple of students."

Principle Hines narrowed his eyes at Erin. "Well you know that is not how we do things around here, so let's not have another incident like this again, ok?"

"Yes Sir."

Principle Hines turned and walked away and then David and Erin left also.

Lauren looked over at me. "Wow that was entertaining. Erin is pretty wound up about all of this."

I nodded my head at Lauren. "Yes, it seems that he has a personal vendetta out against Luke and his friends."

The bell rang.

CHAPTER 5
ARIEL AND LUKE

I stood at Ariel's bedside watching her sleep. I had been doing this for the last few days, but didn't understand why? There was something about her pale white face surrounded by her beautiful red hair that tore right through me. I was beginning to see what Alexander found so very attractive about this human. I heard the door open behind me and turned around, it was Darla.

Darla quickly moved to my side. "What are you doing in here again, Luke?"

I shook my head sideways at her. "What do you want Darla?"

Darla looked down at Ariel as she lay in the bed sleeping. "Answer my question Luke. You like her don't you?"

I laughed. "You are crazy Darla I am just protecting our investment."

Darla narrowed her eyes at me. "I know you Luke, it is more than that. We didn't need Ariel for this and you know it. We could have killed Ariel and brought Antoinette to Calicia and got the same thing out of Alexander."

"It wouldn't have worked like that Darla. Alexander and Antoinette are smart."

"It would have worked but instead you wanted Ariel with us, you are obsessed with this red headed human. I should just kill her now!"

I looked at Darla and could feel my eyes glowing. "Get out Darla!"

Darla looked shocked and then turned and walked out of Ariel's room.

I walked closer to Ariel's bed and bent over her. "Wake up Ariel, wake up."

I heard Luke's voice as I opened my eyes. Once they were open, I saw him looking down at me. I blinked a couple of times and tried to lean up but couldn't.

"Just lay still for a few moments Ariel, you lost a lot of blood and are probably still a little dizzy."

I was lying on a huge bed. I tried to sit up again, this time successfully. "Where am I Luke?"

"You are in Canada."

I felt some stinging pain in my right arm and when I looked down I saw a small bandage around the inner part of my elbow. "Had I been cut? Had I been bitten?" I wondered. The last thing I remembered was being in my apartment and then Luke showing up and then the feel of Luke's hand as it spread across my face. I touched the bandage.

Luke looked down at it. "Yes, it was necessary."

I looked up at Luke. "What did you do to me?" He didn't answer. "I am serious Luke tell me what's going on? Am I a vam…..?"

Luke laughed. "Are you what, a vampire?"

"Yes," I said my voice barely a whisper.

"Relax teacher, you are still human, you would know if you had been changed, trust me. Didn't Alexander explain anything to you?"

I put my head down.

Luke laughed again. "Ah, my guess is correct. Alexander hasn't told you much about vampires, has he?"

"No."

"As I said, you are still human but I must admit Ariel that it was very difficult to be around your blood like that. It is so appealing to me and it took a lot of restraint, even using a syringe. We almost lost you there for a moment."

"Why did you take my blood?"

"Let me just say that I left an urgent message in your apartment for Alexander and I needed him to take it seriously."

I turned my head from side to side and looked around the room. I was in a log cabin and it looked immaculate. I lay on a huge four poster log bed, the room had a big stone fireplace and a fire burned brightly in it. There were antique dressers and chests, a rocking chair and two chairs and a reading table that sat near the fireplace. The plank flooring had been covered with rugs. I didn't see a lamp anywhere and when I looked up to the ceiling there were no light fixtures. "No lights?"

Luke shook his head at me. "No electricity Ariel, we are in the middle of no where. I am afraid you will have to make due with the light from the fireplace and the candles."

"But this looks like a ten million dollar cabin, is there running water?"

Luke smiled. "It is a ten million dollar cabin, and there is water, from a well".

"Where are we?"

"I told you, somewhere in Canada and that is all you need to know. Don't think about trying to escape teacher, the cabin sits on the top of a massive cliff with sharp jagged rocks all the way down to the bottom. The only way to reach it is to rock climb five hundred feet or come in by helicopter."

"You are joking right?"

Luke laughed. "Do I look like the joking type? My father had it built on top of this rock for a purpose. He had the contractor and the logs flown in by helicopter. It took forever to build, being built by humans I mean, but it is truly in the middle of no where."

"But surely people know it is here?"

Luke shook his head at me. "How, there are no utilities, and no road that leads to it. This cabin sits twenty miles from the nearest road, another reason that you wouldn't want to try an escape. Canada has some huge timber wolves and even if you managed to climb five-hundred feet down the rocks, you wouldn't make it twenty miles in this wilderness to the nearest road."

My heart sank. I wondered how Alexander would ever find me.

Luke reached out to touch my face and I turned away. "Sorry about the bruise on your face, I really didn't mean to hit you that hard. Sometimes I don't know my own strength."

I touched my cheek, it was sore. "Yes, Luke I am sure that you are sorry. Now are you going to tell me why I am here?"

Luke shook his head. "Teacher, teacher so many questions, you are the student now."

I raised my voice at him. "Luke, I want to go home now."

Luke laughed. "Seriously, Ariel, you can be so funny at times. I suggest that you enjoy your stay until Alexander shows up and brings me what I want."

My heart leaped as Luke's words rang in my head, Alexander, was coming. I looked at Luke. "I am not afraid of you."

"Yes, I sensed that about you Ariel but you had better do as I say. You need to keep your voice down and maintain a low profile you are in a house with thirty other vampires. This is my departed father's coven, now under the rule of my wicked stepmother. You will meet Calicia shortly and here is a vital tip to your survival, don't make her angry. She is not a vampire that you want to play with."

"I am not leaving this room Luke unless I go home."

"Ariel, the next place you are going is downstairs to meet Calicia and you had better take heed to what I told you. Come on, get up lets go."

Luke attempted to take my arm and I jerked it free from him. "I need to use the bathroom and freshen up a bit."

Luke pointed to a door. "Through that door, I will wait for you here."

I got up from the bed and walked away from Luke and through the door that he had pointed to. It was a small bathroom with a shower but it would do while I was being held captive. Luke's words rang out in my head, "I suggest that you enjoy your stay until Alexander shows up and brings me what I want." I wondered what Luke wanted from Alexander? Was it the vampire anesthesia? And then I realized that it was either that or Alexander and Antoinette's secret about how they could change a vampire back to being a human. I would cost Alexander and Antoinette their life's work. Now I understood what Alexander meant that night in my room when he had told me that I didn't realize the danger's involved in dating a vampire. His secret was at jeopardy because of me and I knew that Alexander would do anything to save me. I saw some plastic cups on the sink and filled one with water and drank it, I felt dehydrated. I felt dizzy for a moment and realized that I hadn't eaten in a while. I washed my face and brushed through my hair with a hairbrush that was lying on the counter and walked back out into the bedroom. "I am still a little dizzy I think I need to eat something".

"In a while Ariel, follow me. There is just one more thing that is really important."

"What is it?"

"Calicia does not know that I have been in Oregon and she doesn't know where you are from either. It is better for both of us if she doesn't find out."

I looked at him inquisitively. "Why, what does it matter?"

"You will see when you meet her, but trust me, the less she knows the better. She isn't a vampire that you would want to know where you live, if you get what I mean. If she asks you, just tell her you are from California."

I saw the seriousness in Luke's eyes and although I didn't trust him by any means, for some reason I trusted him on this issue. "Ok."

Luke opened up the bedroom door. "Come on Ariel, follow me."

I followed him out of the bedroom and down a long hallway, there were other doorways in the hallway that I assumed were bedrooms, I counted eight. We walked down a staircase and to another level so I assumed we had been on the third level of the cabin. "How many stories does this cabin have?"

"It is three stories high."

I had been correct. The second level was a huge loft that overlooked a huge great room, down below. It had a massive stone fireplace and both side walls were glass that went from the floor all the way to the ceiling. "This is amazing."

Luke laughed. "Yes."

I looked out one of the glass walls while we descended from the second level to the first and saw what Luke meant about the steepness and jaggedness of the rocks. We were definitely on top of a cliff and it went straight down, we were so high that I couldn't even see the bottom of the rocks. Once we reached the bottom of the stairs I followed Luke down a hallway and into the huge great room of the cabin.

Luke turned to face me. "Now remember what I said teacher, keep your mouth shut."

I didn't reply.

A moment later a tall blonde haired, blue eyed woman walked into the room, she was accompanied by two very tall and muscular men who stood on each side of her and probably obeyed her every command. They both had long black hair and dark eyes and were toned, they looked like male models, "Body guards," I thought. Calicia was dressed immaculately in a dark blue low cut evening gown accompanied by an excessive amount of diamonds in the form of a choker, multiple rings and a huge pair of earrings.

Luke walked over and stood in front of Calicia and addressed the body guards, "Hello Fredricko and Antoinio." Next he addressed Calicia, "Calicia meet Ariel."

Before I could even blink my eyes she moved and stood in front of me. She was almost six foot tall with her heels on. She took her index finger and touched the tip of my chin and pushed my head upward. "So, this is the bait."

Luke quickly moved and stood next to her. "Yes, Calicia this is Ariel."

"What could a male vampire possibly see in this?"

She talked as if I weren't even there. "Excuse you Calicia?"

Calicia seemed surprised that I had made the remark. "So, she is not only short, but she is stupid as well."

I pushed her finger off of my chin and took a step backwards. "You need to learn some manners lady."

Luke stepped in front of me. "Ariel, shut up."

Calicia smiled at me. "Yes Ariel, listen to Luke and curb that little tongue of yours before I bite it out."

All of a sudden her face changed. Her eyes glowed and she had fangs that hung out over the edges of her bottom lip and her face just seemed to stretch long ways down. She stepped closer to me and opened her mouth. Her jaw retracted in a forward motion, like when a shark is about ready to chomp down on something, she looked hideous. I thought I was going to die, but I just froze and couldn't move. I think my lack of action startled her.

Her face retracted back to normal and she moved away from me. "So, you are not afraid of me Ariel?"

I looked directly at her. "I am not afraid to die, if that is what you mean? I will go to heaven."

Calicia laughed. "Ah! What a marvelous concept."

Luke stood next to me and I turned my head toward him. "Why did she look like that?"

Luke looked surprised for a moment. "Because that's what vampires look like, do you think that we always look like every day people? The fangs and those eyes and her face, that's what vampires really look like. That's right Ariel that is what your precious Alexander looks like, haven't you seen him like that before?"

I put my head down momentarily and then raised it up again. "No."

"Well how would you feel about him if he looked like that all the time? Would you still love him then?"

"Yes."

"Your ridiculous Ariel, you would not."

"I would, I don't care what he looks like! I know what is inside of him."

Luke laughed loudly at me. "Nothing is inside of him he is a soulless, lifeless creature, just like us."

"He is nothing like any of you and never will be!"

Calicia stepped toward me again. "Oh, but you are wrong my dear. The Alexander that I seek I can assure you, is very old and his trail of carnage is quite lengthy."

I snapped out my response at her. "But he doesn't kill anymore, he told me so."

Calicia laughed. "He lied to you, he feeds with his sister occasionally or didn't he tell you that?"

"No, he doesn't!" She was confusing me I didn't know what to believe.

Calcia had her eyes fixed on me. "Now tell me what you know about this Alexander and his secrets?"

"I don't know anything."

All of a sudden she extended her arm and quickly with the tip of her bright red finger nail she raked it across my shoulder.

"Ouch," I screamed and stepped away from her and then all of a sudden and to my surprise Luke stepped in front of me.

"That's enough Calicia." I stepped in front of Ariel and reacted so quickly that I didn't realize what I had done. It surprised me. I turned my head from Calicia to Ariel. "Come with me Ariel lets get you back up to your room." I pushed Ariel in front of me. "Go." As I walked out of the room I could hear Calcia laughing wildly.

"Lukas, you have a soft spot for the human, how very touching."

Luke walked in front of me and led the way up the staircase to the second floor, then to the third floor and down the hallway to the door of my room.

Luke unlocked the door. "You will be safe in here."

"Thank you. I am really hungry." I stepped into the room.

"I will bring you something to eat and drink in a few minuets." Luke closed the door and I heard him lock it.

* * *

I left Ariel in her room and walked down the hallway. Darla approached me. "Darla, what are you doing up here? I told you to wait in our room."

"Luke, what was that all about?"

I shook my head at her. "Were you spying on me Darla? I told you to stay with Matt and Jason in our room until I got back."

Darla rolled her eyes at me. "We were getting bored."

"Don't you mean worried. What did you think that I was going to take the money from Calicia and leave without all of you?"

Darla shrugged her shoulders. "After seeing you with Ariel, I am not sure what you might do. You seem to be a little too obsessed with her these days."

I laughed at her. "You are crazy Darla."

"I know you Luke. I saw you downstairs when Calicia scratched Ariel. You were ready to fight and defend her."

"Shut up Darla, I was just protecting my investment."

"Sure Luke and we are protecting ours. You promised us money too, remember?"

"I remember Darla, now get back to the room and stay there with Matt and Jason and wait for me." Darla turned and left.

* * *

Luke had left me in my room and I sat in a chair by the fireplace. I looked at the scratch on my shoulder, it wasn't too deep, just a surface scratch. I knew that Calicia could have inflicted a much worse wound if she had wanted to. I just couldn't get the image of her face out of my head and what Luke said about how vampires looked like that and how Alexander also looked like that. I couldn't picture Alexander looking that wicked. I couldn't picture him looking any different than he looked now, but I knew that Luke had told me the truth. Luke was right, I knew very little about vampires. A knock at the door interrupted my thoughts. "Who is it?"

"Ariel, it is Luke, open the door. I have brought you some food."

I got up from the chair and walked over to the door and unlocked it. Luke stood in the doorway with a tray of food. I opened the door wider and he walked in and over to a table near the fireplace and set the tray down.

"I thought that vampires didn't eat food?"

"We don't, but occasionally Calicia entertains a human or two and she provides them with an awesome last meal, being that they usually end up as the desert. She believes in the best of everything, so here you go." Luke took the cover off of the tray. "Lobster, pasta and champagne, it will have to do."

"I am starving, thanks. So how do you have refrigeration without electricity?"

"We have generators that provide power when there is not enough sun shine to power the solar power panels. Why do you ask so many questions Ariel?"

"Just curious, that's all. It does look really good."

I looked at Ariel. There was something very different about her when compared to other human females. She seemed very childish and innocent.

I sat down in a chair at the table and began to eat.

"The bruise on your face is almost gone. I am sorry about hitting you but it was in your best interest."

I stopped eating and looked up at him as he stood near the table. "What do you mean?"

"Well it was safer for you to be unconscious, I mean around Darla, Matt and Jason. Darla is not very fond of you."

"Why isn't she? I have never done anything to her."

Luke laughed. "It is not that Ariel, I mean she is just being Darla."

I continued eating. "So Luke, this is your home? It is very lovely."

Luke lowered his head. "It was my home once, when my father was alive but ever since he died it hasn't been the same."

"I am so sorry, when did he pass away?"

Luke raised his head and looked back at me. "It was about sixty years ago, shortly after he met Calica and built this cabin."

"I lost my parents last year in a car accident."

"Sorry....I didn't know – about your parents or I wouldn't have asked you that question that day in class about which parent you got your red hair from."

"Luke, how did your dad die?"

"It was long ago Ariel".

"Tell me, I would like to know".

Luke lowered his head momentarily and then raised it again and looked at me. "My father was killed by a rival vampire coven who invaded our home."

"How awful, I am sorry. You left home after he died?"

Luke shook his head. "No, I stayed for a while. I left here about forty years ago and traveled all over the world and later decided to move to Portland."

"Why did you choose Portland?"

"You ask too many questions Ariel."

"Sorry." I continued eating.

"So what about you Ariel, are you from Portland?"

I stopped eating and looked up at him. "Yes, Portland is home. My parents moved there from Washington before I was born."

"So, did you attend Lincoln High?"

I laughed. "Oh, no I attended Catholic School all twelve years." I continued eating.

Luke smiled. "How intriguing, I guess my first assumption about you was correct, very innocent indeed and very religious? You really are like Selene the young virgin girl in the story that you told in class, the one that Ambrogio met at the temple in Greece." I watched as Ariel put her head down. "I am sorry I didn't mean to embarrass you."

I looked up at Luke and smiled. "It is ok Luke. I would just rather not talk about that subject, if you don't mind."

All of a sudden I saw in Ariel what Alexander must see in her. She was kind and loving and very gentle. I had a pang of regret for having brought her here and it surprised me. I hadn't felt regret in a long time and for one second it reminded me of who I used to be, a southern gentleman in the eighteen-hundreds.

"So Luke would you mind if I ask you a personal question?"

"What's that Ariel?"

"When were you born?"

Luke laughed.

I persisted. "No, really Luke I would like to know."

Luke smiled. "Ok Ariel.......I was born in eighteen-fifty-five."

"Wow that is so amazing. What did you do back then, I mean your profession?"

"Really Ariel, none of this is important."

"Please…I want to know."

"My father was in the military and I was being groomed to be an Officer in the military."

"Really, how exciting. What happened?"

The smile faded from Luke's face. "This happened."

I knew what he meant. "You were changed."

"Yes my father first, then me."

"What about your mother?" After I asked the question I could tell by the look on Luke's face that this was a difficult subject for him to talk about.

"She had died several years before that is enough questions Ariel."

"Just one more please?"

"What is it?"

"Tell me what it was like between a man and a woman back then?"

Ariel had touched on a subject that I hadn't thought about in many years. "I don't think I can remember."

I looked at Luke and saw that he was trying to avoid my question. "Really Luke, what was it like?"

"Ok, Ariel if you really want to know, it was very simple. A man was a man and a woman was a woman."

"What do you mean?"

"Well a woman was taken care of, protected and provided for. She was revered as someone that was precious and very important to her husband and family."

I smiled at him. "I bet you were a real southern gentleman Luke?"

"Yes, once upon a time."

"Why can't things be like that now Luke?"

I looked at Ariel and for the first time in a long time I really smiled. "I wish things were like that Ariel, but they aren't. I have to go I will check on you later."

"Thanks again for the dinner Luke." Luke left the room.

CHAPTER 6
THE RESCUE

While I drove I turned my head sideways to my brother. "Alexander? How much further is it to the Canadian border?" He looked distracted and I knew that he was thinking about Ariel.

"The border is about two miles away, try and find a place to pull over." Alexander turned his head back to Zack, Jeremy and Mia as they sat in the back seat. "Antoinette and I are the only two that have passports. It is dark now so we will let you guys out along side the road, find a place to cross the border, where you won't be seen and then catch back up with us on the other side."

Zack leaned up in his seat. "No problem Alexander."

Alexander pointed to the side of the road. "Antoinette, that looks like a good spot over there."

I pulled the Hummer off the road to where he had pointed to and brought it to a stop. Zack, Jeremy and

Mia quickly got out. I rolled my window down. "See you guys in a few minuets."

"Later." Zack replied and then they disappeared into the woods.

I resumed driving and a few minuets later approached the check point at the border. I slowed the Hummer down and stopped and then rolled my window down to greet the Border Patrol Officer. "Good evening, Officer."

He approached the vehicle and stopped at my window. "Good evening Ma'am, your passports please?"

Alexander handed me his passport and I handed both of the passports to the Officer.

He examined them and then returned them to me. "What is your reason for visiting Canada Ma'am?"

I smiled at him. "Does one need a reason to visit one of the most beautiful countries in the world?"

He liked my answer and smiled back at me. "No Ma'am you certainly don't. Enjoy your stay and I hope that I am on duty when you leave Canada so that I will have the pleasure of seeing your beautiful face one more time."

"Thank you," I said and rolled the window up and resumed driving.

Alexander looked over at me and shook his head. "Smooth, sister I see that you haven't lost your touch."

"Well I certainly hope not, whatever would I do if I did?" Alexander laughed and it felt good to see him smile, even though it only lasted for a second.

All of a sudden I heard a huge thud on the rooftop and knew that Zack, Jeremy and Mia had rejoined us. I rolled the rear windows of the Hummer down and they climbed in.

"Well that didn't take too long," I said.

"Nope, we ran at warp speed," Zack said and laughed.

"Did you encounter any problems?" Alexander asked.

Zack laughed. "Just a few timber wolves that we ran into along the way, but they moved out of our path pretty quick."

I turned my head slightly sideways as I drove. "There are some fresh bags of blood in the cooler, I suggest we all feed to keep up our strength up."

"Thanks Antoinette, I was getting Hungry," Mia said.

Jeremy reached back and opened up the cooler and passed out the bags.

I looked back at Jeremy. "Jeremy there is a box of straws inside the cooler, would you please get one for me?"

"Sure thing, here you go Antoinette," he said and handed me a straw.

I took the straw from him. "Thanks Jeremy. Alexander how much further is it?"

"Not too much further, we should see County Road 234 up ahead. We are to turn right onto it and then follow it up to the base of the mountain. Luke said that we will see a garage and we are to park there and continue up the mountain on foot."

"I see a turn coming up Alexander." I read the sign, County Road 234, "This is it." I turned the Hummer off the highway and onto the road and continued to drive. It was a heavily wooded area and the road winded around the side of a mountain. We drove for several miles.

Alexander turned his head toward Zack, Jeremy and Mia. "I just thought about something else, you guys should get out of the Hummer before we get to the garage just in case they are watching us when we pull up. Antoinette, pull over there." Alexander pointed to a spot alongside the road.

I did as my brother asked and slowed the Hummer down and then brought it to a stop.

Alexander continued talking to them. "Follow behind the Hummer and then wait near the garage for Antoinette to return with Ariel."

Zack opened his door. "You got it Alexander, come on Jeremy, Mia let's go."

They all three got out of the Hummer and I continued driving. "That was probably a good idea Alexander." He didn't comment, I could tell that his mind was preoccupied with his plan.

Alexander pointed to a huge log garage. "There, over there Antoinette, that must be it!"

I looked at the massive building. "Yes, it certainly fits Luke's description. He hadn't exaggerated when he said it was big, it probably holds ten vehicles." I pulled the Hummer up to the garage and turned the engine off. We climbed out. I looked over at my brother. "Ok, now what?"

Alexander glanced upward at the mountain and then pointed. "Up there, there is the cabin."

I extended my head upward and stretched my neck outward, even with my vision as a vampire I could barely see the speck of a cabin that Alexander referred to. "Luke didn't exaggerate about the cabin either."

"No, he didn't, it is a bit of a climb are you up for it Antoinette?"

I saw Alexander smile as he looked down at my rock climbing shoes he was making fun of me. "You know I am. Should we bring any of the injectors with us?"

"No, leave everything in the Hummer."

Just then I sensed Zack, Jeremy and Mia's presence. "Zack, Jeremy and Mia are here, over there in the trees."

"Good, they can watch the Hummer." Alexander smiled at me. "Ready."

"I am ready." We began our climb upward and I held a position just behind Alexander. It was sharp jagged edged rock the entire way up but we handled it expertly. Each stride that we took moving at warp speed put us on top of another sharp edged bolder. We continued to leap upward from one rock to another and finally reached the base of the cabin. We reached upward and grabbed the railing of the deck and swung ourselves up-ward firmly landing on its wooden surface. I stood looking at the huge log cabin. Its exterior was immacu-late. It stood three stories high and must have at least ten-thousand square foot of space. "Wow, Alexander this is amazing."

"Yes, shall we ring the bell?"

Alexander's tone was condescending but I knew that it was just a way to mask his concern for the situation.

"After you brother". I followed him up to the double wide wooden doors. There was no doorbell so he knocked. The door was opened by two male vampires, they looked like henchmen – "Servants of Calicia," I mumbled to Alexander.

Alexander smiled.

"I am Tony and this is Fredricko."

I am Alexander Von-Allenberg and this is my sister Antoinette. I believe Calicia Claig is expecting us.

Tony opened the door wider. "Yes, please come in and follow us."

I followed Alexander through the doorway and into the foyer. I looked at the interior of the cabin and it was more immaculate and impressive than the exterior was. The logs were all exposed on the inside and the floors were marbled. It was decorated with an old charm of rustic Germany and it made me wonder if Calcia Claig was of German decent. We followed Tony and Fredricko down a long hallway and emerged into the great room of the cabin. The great room had triple vaulted ceilings and a massive rock fireplace and was surrounded by glass walls on two sides. There was a small group of vampires standing near the fireplace talking, I saw Luke among them. He walked away from the group and moved toward us.

"Ah, at last, the infamous Alexander and his little sister have arrived."

Alexander walked toward him. "Save the sarcasm Luke, where is Ariel?"

"If you prefer Alexander, Oh where are my manners? I see that you have already met Tony and Fredricko." Luke turned his head slightly and pointed to a tall blonde vampire who had her back to us. "Alexander and Antoinette meet Calicia Claig."

Just as Luke made the introductions Calicia turned to greet us and then moved quickly to Luke's side. She was quite beautiful, tall, blonde, blue eyed and dressed exquisitely. She wore a designer evening gown and I recognized it immediately. It was an Italian, a Lambichi design. I had always considered my self a collector of clothes but for the first time in my life I was actually a bit jealous of someone else's wardrobe.

Calicia extended her hand out to shake Alexander's hand. "I am pleased to meet you Alexander," she said and shook his hand and then extended her hand toward me. "And I am pleased to meet you too Antoinette." She gripped my hand and held it momentarily and I felt the cruelty in her touch.

She half smiled. "Please sit down we have business to discuss."

Alexander continued his death stare with Luke as he answered Calicia. "No thank you, I want to see Ariel now."

Calicia didn't like his response. "There is no need to be rude Alexander, please humor me and take a seat. I assure you that Ariel is fine, she is resting now."

I watched Alexander move toward the couch and I followed him. We sat down. Calicia and Luke followed us and sat down in chairs that faced the couch.

Alexander persisted. "Where is Ariel?"

Calicia smiled at him. "All in good time Alexander I believe that you have something that I want."

"Yes, Calicia but you won't get it until I get Ariel and until she is safely away from here."

"Yes Alexander, Luke told me that you were quite stubborn, I see what he means."

Alexander maintained a stern face. "Call it what you want, those are my terms and they are not negotiable."

The corners of Calicia's mouth cringed slightly upward. "And what if I don't want to do things your way? What if I decide to kill you right here, right now, you, Antoinette and Ariel."

Alexander laughed at her. "Go ahead, do what you will, but then you wouldn't get what you want, now would you?"

"Ah! Alexander the negotiator, I must admit you are starting to live up to Luke's description."

I saw Alexander glance at Luke and a short snarling sound escaped his throat. For a split second it looked like Luke was afraid. Alexander re-composed himself and turned back to Calicia. "I want to see Ariel now."

Calicia threw her hands up in the air. "Oh Alright Alexander, I never understood what this obsession was that some vampires have with these humans. Luke will you fetch his little pet, so that we can get on with our business."

Alexander glared at Calicia. I knew my brother pretty well it looked like he wanted to rip her head off. Luke got up and left the room.

Calicia just stared at us while Luke was gone. From the top of her head to the tips of her stiletto heels she was perfect. Even the color of her nail polish matched what she was wearing. "Do you mind if I ask where you got your dress from?"

"Not at all Antoinette, it is from Paris."

I was confused. "But it is Italian?"

Calicia smiled. "Oh, I am impressed you follow the fashion world. Yes you are correct it is a "Lambichi" but I have a good friend who lives in Paris and it was a gift from him."

I walked into the great room with Luke and I saw Alexander and Antoinette – sitting on the couch. Alexander turned his head to me and then jumped from the couch at warp speed and wrapped his arms around me. He kissed me. "Ariel, Ariel. Are you ok?"

I rested my head on his shoulder. "Oh! Alexander I am so sorry."

"Don't be sorry, I am just glad that you are un-harmed."

I looked up at him and smiled. "Alexander, this is totally my fault, can you ever forgive me?" Before I knew what was happening I felt Luke's arms on me and he yanked me away from Alexander and pulled me to his side.

Calicia Claig's voice rang out throughout the cabin. "Enough of the lover's mish mash."

Alexander looked like he was ready to rip Luke's head off, but instead he yelled out to me. "Ariel we are going to get you out of here."

Calicia stood from the couch. "Alright Alexander you have what you want now give me what I want."

Alexander stepped toward Calcia. "And so I shall, right after you let Antoinette and Ariel leave."

Calicia retorted. "Not so fast Alexander, you don't think I am going to let anyone leave until I get what I want. I want the medicine that makes vampires sleep."

"You have it already."

Calicia looked confused. "What do you mean Alexander?"

Alexander stepped closer to Calcia. "You have me, what you desire is locked away in my head. I am the only one who knows the formula, it is my invention."

Alexander was going to trade himself to save me! My head started spinning. "No, Alexander you can't, you mustn't."

Calicia looked as though she was analyzing the situation. "An interesting proposal Alexander but I have an even better one. I don't want what's in your head I want a sample of the finished product, the medicine, so here is my counterproposal. I will hold on to your little sister until you bring me what I want. You and Ariel may leave."

Alexander's eyes burned with anger. "No you won't," he said.

I recognized the tone of my brother's voice and the look on his face, his fangs were about ready to extract and he was about to loose it. I stepped between him and Calicia Claig. "Stop it Alexander." I turned to Calcia

Claig. "Fine I will stay and Alexander will take Ariel, he will return with what you want."

Calicia smiled at me. "What a devoted little sister you are, how precious, agreed. Alexander you and your pet may leave, but I wouldn't dawdle if I were you. The clock is ticking, tick tock, tick tock, hurry back."

Antoinette would give herself to save me! I saw the pain in Alexander's face and it killed me. I had put Antoinette's life in jeopardy and somehow I didn't think that Alexander would ever forgive me for this.

My brother was distraught. I quickly moved to his side and whispered in his ear. "Leave now Alexander and get Ariel out of here."

Alexander turned his head to me. "Antoinette I can't leave you here."

"Alexander, you must." I wrapped my arms around my brother's neck and pulled his forehead to meet mine. "I love you Alexander, you can do this. Do it for me, for everything we have accomplished together." I had never seen this much anguish in his face before, if a vampire could cry he would have. "Please just go now."

Alexander speed to Ariel's side and took her by the arm and walked out of the room. "Come on Ariel."

Alexander ushered me out of the great room and down a long hallway to the front door and then outside onto a large wooden deck and over to the railing.

"Alexander I am sorry I am so sorry."

He continued moving. "Not now Ariel."

In one swooping motion Alexander grabbed me and flung me on his back. "Hold on tight, it is a long way down."

"We are going down there?" I said looking over Alexander's shoulder at the steep drop below.

"Yes, close your eyes."

I closed my eyes and felt as if I were flying through the air but that feeling did not last long when I felt the heavy thud that followed. We landed, on a rock I guessed and then we were flying downward again, spiraling through the air so fast that I couldn't even count to one before I felt the impact of another landing. This form of travel continued for a few minuets until I heard Alexander tell me to open my eyes. I did. We were on flat ground.

"Ariel, are you alright?"

"Yes I think so."

I stepped away from Ariel. "Zack, Jeremy?"

Zack, Jeremy and Mia emerged from the trees and Zack moved to my side. "Alexander, where is Antoinette, is she ok?"

I turned my head to Zack. "Calicia Claig has her. We have to get back there fast." I saw Jeremy shoot Zack an unusual look and I sensed that something was wrong. "What's wrong Jeremy?"

Jeremy turned his head to me. "It's nothing Alexander, just a premonition that Zack had about Antoinette a while back."

I shook my head at him. "Don't tell me about it now. We need to hurry back to get Antoinette. Jeremy, take Ariel with you like we discussed."

"Ok Alexander, Ariel come with me please, we need to go now!"

Jeremy moved to my side and I wanted to scream out, no I am not leaving, but I didn't. They had all sacrificed so much to rescue me. Jeremy took me by the arm.

"Let's go Ariel now."

I followed Jeremy to the Hummer and got in the passenger seat. Jeremy got in the driver's seat.

"Ariel put your seat belt on."

Jeremy started the Hummer up and backed it away from the garage and we sped down the road. I turned my head back to look through the rear window as we drove away and saw Alexander looking at me.

"Ariel before we get to the Canadian and US border we must stop and I have to get out."

"Why?"

"Because they will check for passports and identification and I don't have either."

"Either do I, I don't have my purse."

"Your purse is in the back seat Antoinette brought it from your apartment."

I turned slightly in my seat and looked into the back seat and saw my purse laying there, I grabbed it. I was barely hearing what Jeremy was saying, I felt as if everything was happening in slow motion. I was so worried about Alexander and the others. If they died it would be my fault. I opened my purse to make sure that my wallet was in it, it was.

"After you cross the border I will rejoin you?"

"I don't have my cell phone, how will I get in touch with you?"

Jeremy laughed. "No worries. You will hear me when I jump on the top of the Hummer, don't be alarmed just roll the window down for me."

"Ok."

CHAPTER 7
THE FIGHT

Calicia and I sat in the great room of the cabin. I sat on the couch and she sat in a chair across from me. I looked over at her. "I really do like that dress. You must be well connected in the fashion world because you can't buy that dress on the open market it is only for friends of friends of the designer."

Calicia smiled. "Yes, I am well connected. It appears that you share my love of expensive clothing. What size are you, let me guess a size two?"

I nodded my head at her. "Yes."

"I hope that brother of yours doesn't take too long to return I would hate to have to dispose of you, to tell the truth I rather like you."

I laughed. "Ditto, and the stiletto shoes that you are wearing I don't recognize the design by name, what is it called?"

"It is a Calicia?"

"I don't understand?"

"It was made by the designer just for me."

"Wow." This woman was making me insanely jealous of her wardrobe!

* * *

Antoinette had been with Calicia for a half hour now and I was worried sick. I climbed the mountain leaping upward one rock at a time with Zack at my side and Mia behind me. We finally reached the base of the cabin and stood up. I turned to Zack. "Ok, Zack you take the third floor of the cabin and Mia and I will start on the second floor, we will meet on the ground floor."

"Ok Alexander." In one leap Zack jumped toward the roof and landed firmly on it.

I turned to Mia. "Come on Mia, we will crawl along the foundation of the cabin, around the side of it and then up the wall to the second floor."

Mia moved to my side. "Alright Alexander, I am right behind you."

I led the way and slowly moved along the foundation of the cabin and around the corner to a side wall, we stopped. I looked upward and saw a drain pipe above us, next to a window. "Ok, we are going up that drain pipe and through the window, as quietly as possible." I began ascending upward using the drain pipe like a staircase railing and when I was eye level with the window I looked through it, it was a bedroom and there was no one in it. I pushed the window open and climbed in and then Mia came in after me.

Mia looked nervous. "Ok Alexander, now what?"

"Keep quiet and stay behind me. Everything will be ok and remember, use the injectors if you need them."

Mia nodded her head at me. "I will Alexander."

I walked to the door and opened it and looked out into the hallway, there was no one in sight. I stepped out into the hallway and Mia followed behind me. Just then another door opened and one of Calicia's vampires stepped out.

He turned his head to me. "What are you doing up here?"

I moved at warp speed to his side and he reacted in a way as to defend himself. I quickly stuck him with an injector. As quickly as I did I felt another set of hands on me and realized that another vampire had hold of me. Out of the corner of my eye I saw Mia struggling with a third vampire. The noise of us crashing into walls and into hallway tables surely had alerted the rest of the house that something was wrong. I looked at Mia and saw that she was about to loose her fight. I pulled myself away from the vampire that had a hold on me and turned and then dropped to the ground. He hadn't expected that, I leapt upward and locked my arms around his head and snapped it off. I quickly flung myself onto the vampire that had hold of Mia's head and locked my arms around his head and snapped it backwards. It had been many years since I had killed another creature and I had forgotten what it felt like, it did not feel good.

Mia looked over at me. "Thank you Alexander, I thought I was going to die."

"You are doing ok Mia."

Two more vampires entered the hallway and I briefly wondered how Zack was doing on the third floor all alone.

Mia leapt forward onto one of the vampires. "I got this one Alexander."

The second vampire lunged for me but I evaded her attack by twisting my body sideways and then jumping upward into the air. I bounced off the ceiling and back downward right on top of her and locked my arms around her neck and snapped her head forward, it rolled to the floor. I looked over at Mia and she was still battling with the male vampire. I was just about to intervene when I saw the vampire slump to the floor.

Mia sighed heavily. "Finally, I put someone to sleep

with my gift. I really need to practice this more."

I laughed. "You will get the hang of it."

We moved quickly down the hallway toward the staircase and were met by three more vampires.

"Alexander, I got him," Mia yelled out.

The other two vampires faced me and I knew that in order to beat both of them I would have to kill them quickly. I jumped straight up in the air and landed directly between them. I wrapped my arms around their necks and knocked their heads together and then squeezed tightly. They twisted and used their arms to try and remove my arms from around their necks, I kicked their legs out from under them and the weight of their own bodies helped me to snap their heads off. I stepped away from them.

Mia just stood there starring at me. "Alexander that was awesome I have never seen anything like that ever in my life."

"Thank you Mia. Antoinette and I both have a lot of fighting experience. Let's go." I walked toward the staircase that led to the ground floor and Mia followed me.

* * *

I heard the noise upstairs and knew that it was Alexander and the others. Calicia jumped from her chair and stood by the fireplace with Tony at her side, he was ready to defend her. All of a sudden I heard Luke's voice and looked up. He stood in the doorway accompanied by Darla, Matt and Jason. They were holding back packs and tote bags.

Luke smiled at Calicia. "Calicia I will be leaving you now, thanks for the hospitality and for all of your money."

At first Calicia looked shocked but then she glared at Luke. "Come back here with my money."

Luke smiled at her. "It is my father's money, hence my money, it was never yours".

Calicia yelled out at him. "I will get you for this Lukas, if it is the last thing that I ever do."

Luke laughed and then he and his friends quickly disappeared.

I heard Alexander call out to me and then heard Calicia scream to Tony. "Tony, kill her."

Tony lunged toward me and I jumped up in the air. He leaped upward and grabbed me and threw me to the floor. I rolled and stood up and then jumped into the air and landed on top of him with my feet resting on each side of his hips. I straddled him and grabbed his head and began to twist it off. Out of the corner of my eye I saw that Calicia was about ready to pounce on me. I ripped Tony's head off and threw it into the fireplace.

Calicia looked shocked and backed away from me. Just then I heard Alexander call out my name. "Antoinette."

Calicia moved at lightning speed and ran – right through the glass windows out onto the deck.

Alexander, Mia and Zack came into the great room and I followed Calicia out onto the deck. In one leap she went over it and disappeared into the darkness. I ran to the deck railing and called out after her, "Be careful with that dress."

Alexander ran to my side. "Antoinette, are you insane?"

"No I am not. That dress is a Lambichi, it is priceless."

Alexander put his arms around me and hugged me. "Well, it appears that your fashion sense has saved you. I will buy you a Lambichi for Christmas."

I shook my head at him. "Alexander you can't buy that dress on the open market. It is only made for friends of friends of the designer."

Alexander laughed. "We need to get out of here no telling how many more vampires are here. Mia and I took out seven on the second floor. They are dead except for two, one that Mia put to sleep and one that I put to sleep. "What's your count Zack?"

Zack smiled. "When I got up to the third floor, some of the vampires had already been disposed of, but I took out another ten."

"Wow Zack, ten vampires by your self is pretty impressive. Luke must have gotten to the other vampires first. Speaking of Luke, has anyone seen him?"

I looked at my brother. "Yes brother, he was here with Darla, Matt and Jason right before you guys arrived. Luke apparently took all of Calicia's money and they left."

"I should have known he would have been up to something like that, lets get out of here." I led everyone over to the deck railing and we all jumped over it and began climbing down the jagged rocks at warp speed, leaping from one rock to the next. We were almost to the bottom when all of a sudden we heard a loud explosion and stopped. We looked up toward the cabin, it was in flames. "I wonder, what happened?"

I looked at my brother. "Luke happened."

Alexander smiled. "You think he did that?"

I nodded my head at him. "Yes I do." We continued down the mountain and landed safely on the ground near the garage. I looked at my brother. "Ok, Alexander, now what?"

He smiled. "We watch our backs and run for the border. We should be able to catch up with Jeremy and Ariel just after they cross it."

"After you Alexander," Zack said.

Alexander led the way followed by Zack, Mia and I. We ran into the darkness.

* * *

"Ariel, we are getting close to the border I am going to pull over."

"Ok Jeremy."

I pulled the Hummer over to the side of the road and opened my door and got out. Ariel got out of the passenger side and walked around the Hummer and got into the driver's seat.

"Jeremy I am so nervous. I don't know if I can do this. What if they want to see my passport? I don't have one, I only have my driver's license."

I smiled at her. "It is ok Ariel, calm down. If they ask to see your passport tell them that you lost it while you were on vacation and that you will report it lost as soon as you get home. They will let you cross the border with your driver's license."

"Are you sure?"

"Yes, don't worry. Just stay calm and smile at them."

"Ok Jeremy I will see you in a while."

I left Jeremy on the side of the road and started driving toward the Canadian and US border. In spite of his pep talk I was still nervous, more so about Alexander and the others, I couldn't live with myself if something happened to them. I saw lights up ahead and slowed the Hummer down and then came to a stop. There was a small line of vehicles and it appeared that they were indeed checking everyone's identification. I edged the Hummer slowly up to the border check point and then rolled my window down. A Border Patrol Officer approached.

He stopped at the window. "Good evening Ma'am, can I see your passport?"

"Just my luck he would have to ask for the passport," I thought. I opened my purse and took out my driver's license and handed it to him and then recalled the excuse that Jeremy had told me to use. "I am sorry Officer I lost my passport while on vacation and I am going to report it lost as soon as I get home."

The Officer looked at my driver's license one more time and then at me. I held my breath.

He smiled at me. "Alright Ma'am you do that and have a good evening."

"Thank you Officer, you do the same." He handed me my driver's license back, I put it in my purse and then set my purse in the passenger seat. I put the Hummer in gear and pulled slightly forward and then accelerated to a moderate speed. It just took a few moments before I realized that I was back in the United States. I drove for another mile or so and then all of a sudden I heard a huge thud on the roof. It scared me at first, but then I realized that it must be Jeremy, or so I hoped. I rolled the passenger window down. "Oh, thank goodness it is you. I almost had a heart attack."

Jeremy climbed in the vehicle. "You did good Ariel, here let me take the wheel."

I didn't even realize what had happened Jeremy quickly slid me out of the driver's seat with one arm, while he gripped the steering wheel with his other arm and then positioned himself in the driver's seat. By the time I realized what had happened I was safely seated in the passenger seat. "I will never get used to vampires and how fast you move."

Jeremy laughed. "Put your seat belt on."

I fastened my seat belt. "Jeremy, do you think that they are ok?"

Jeremy didn't answer me right away. "Ariel, I think they are fine and I will tell you why. I know Zack he can be a killing machine. He is big and quick and it wouldn't surprise me if Zack takes out half of that coven before they even know what hit them."

I smiled at him. "I hope you are right Jeremy." I hadn't realized how exhausted I was and before I knew it against my will I felt myself passing out, my head fell backwards toward the headrest and I saw instant black-ness. It was the loud thud on the rooftop that woke me. I screamed out and then heard Jeremy's voice.

"Ariel, it is ok. They are back." Jeremy rolled the rear windows of the Hummer down.

I quickly sat up in my seat and turned my head and watched as Zack and Mia climbed through the windows, next I saw Antoinette. I held my breath then I saw Alexander. He was ok, they were all ok. I started crying.

Alexander leaned up from the back seat. "Jeremy pull the Hummer over, I will drive."

Jeremy pulled the Hummer safely to the side of the road and stopped. He got out of the driver's seat and got into the back of the Hummer. Alexander got out of the rear passenger door and walked around to my door and opened it and I got out. He shut the door. I was still crying. Alexander leaned his head in the window of the vehicle. "Give, Ariel and I a minute," then he took me by the hand and led me to the rear of the vehicle and then took me into his arms. "Ariel everything is ok. You can stop crying now."

I looked up at him. "I can't stop I was so worried about you and Antoinette, about everybody."

"We are fine."

I rubbed the tears from my eyes. "What happened?"

"Well, let's just say that Calicia Claig doesn't have a coven anymore. She does however have one awesome and expensive evening dress, according to Antoinette. She was wearing it when she leaped over the railing of the deck, she escaped. Luke took her money and burned the cabin to the ground just as we left."

I laughed.

"That's better, now let's go home."

"Alexander, can you ever forgive me? I am so sorry that I didn't listen to you. If I hadn't gone back to my apartment none of this would have happened, it appears that I know nothing about vampires."

Alexander smiled. "It is partly my fault too I have kept a lot of the truths about vampires from you. There is a lot more that you need to know. I will rectify that." I smiled at him. Alexander led me back to the Hummer and we got in. I was surprised at how easily Alexander had forgiven me, he loved me but I knew that Antoinette would not forgive me as easily.

CHAPTER 8
BACK HOME

The ride home was tireless but Portland was a welcome sight as we pulled off the interstate. It had been a long trip and I was exhausted. Everyone had been quiet during the ride and I knew that they weren't tired, they were vampires, but I guessed that they were probably hungry. They had expended a lot of energy to rescue me. I knew so little about vampires I didn't even know how often they needed to feed. I needed to learn more about the people that mattered, the most to me, Alexander and Antoinette. Somehow I had to make it up to both of them. I also realized that I hadn't even said thank you, I cleared my throat. "I am sorry you guys we drove all this way and I haven't even said thank you for rescuing me."

Zack responded. "It is ok Ariel, I am sure that it was a terrifying experience for you."

"Yes I am exhausted." I didn't want to tell them that I hadn't really been too scared, for some reason I had felt safe with Luke having been there, and that thought bothered me. A few minutes later we neared the house and Alexander pulled the Hummer into the driveway.

Alexander turned the vehicle off. "Ok everyone, we are home." He got out of the driver's seat and came around and opened my door and scooped me up in his arms. "Come on Ariel, I will take you to your room."

"Really Alexander, I can walk."

"It is ok I will carry you. You have been through a lot and need to rest."

As Alexander carried me toward the house, I realized that I was totally exhausted and my entire body felt as limp as a noodle.

Alexander walked away with Ariel in his arms and I shook my head. I felt that his display of affection was ridiculous but as usual, he went overboard for Ariel. I turned my head to Zack, Jeremy and Mia. "I am going to unpack the Hummer."

Zack stepped toward me. "Do you want some help Antoinette?"

"No Zack, I am good you guys did enough."

"Alright Antoinette, Jeremy and I are going down-town to patrol some of the clubs and rescue some more women in distress." Zack turned and walked toward the garage door and Jeremy followed him.

I laughed. I knew that they were thirsty and wanted to hunt.

Mia walked after them. "Zack, do you mind if I go with you and Jeremy?"

Zack turned around and looked at Mia. "No problem."

I was surprised that Mia had asked to go along. I watched while Zack, Jeremy and Mia walked out of the garage and sped off into the night, and for a split second I wished I were going with them. I was in the mood to munch on a criminal or two.

Alexander walked back into the garage and interrupted my thoughts. I looked over at him. "Where is Ariel?"

"She is in the shower."

Alexander stepped to my side. "I was really worried about leaving you there you know that right?"

I could tell that my brother was upset with himself for having left me with Calicia. "Of course I know that, but it is ok."

Alexander shook his head. "This was different Antoinette, you did it for her for Ariel, and I just want to tell you thank you and that I love you."

I hugged my brother. "I love you too. I hate to bring this up now, but it is as good of time as any. Alexander, the only way to keep Ariel safe and protect our work is to change her."

Alexander stepped back from me. "I can't do that."

"You have to, it is the only answer."

"That isn't the answer it would be a horrible mistake."

"Alexander you know I am right. We can't be with her twenty-four-seven, I mean she will be teaching her classes alone at school and going out to do things on her own."

Alexander sighed. "I know."

"Well, what are you going to do? She might not be so lucky next time."

"Well for starters I am going to ask her to move in here with us, I mean permanently. I was going to talk to you about that. What do you think?"

I didn't answer him immediately. "I have no objection I figured that you would do that, I mean she is here all the time anyway."

Alexander smiled. "Thanks."

I continued to make my point. "But still, Alexander that will only solve part of the problem. The only way to make sure that she is one-hundred percent safe is to change her. We can always change her back later and did you consider the fact that she is aging? We have a lot of work to do for many, many years to come."

"Of course I have thought about that too, but there has to be another way, maybe I could develop something to slow down her aging process?"

My eyes widened and I just stared at my brother. "Are you insane? That is how this all started remember, you trying to discover the fountain of youth and turned yourself into a vampire."

Alexander put his head down. "I know I am sorry." He looked back up at me.

I looked directly into his face. "There is no other way. You need to change her if you want her to be safe."

Alexander turned away from me. "I am going back inside to see Ariel."

Alexander turned and walked out of the garage. My brother truly loved this human enough to die for her and I knew that if Ariel remained a human that something horrible was going to happen. The memory of Kayal surfaced in my mind and I slammed the door of the Hummer so hard that it cracked. "I should have gone hunting with Zack and Jeremy tonight," I thought and all of a sudden I found myself moving to the door of the garage and outside into the darkness to join them.

* * *

I left Antoinette in the garage and walked into the house. I stopped just outside of Ariel's bedroom door and knocked. "Ariel, it is Alexander, may I come in?"

Her voice rang out. "Come in Alexander."

I opened up the door and stepped into the room. Ariel sat in her bed wearing her pajamas. Her red hair was piled on top of her head and her back rested against the headboard. She had a notebook open in front of her.

"What are you doing?"

Ariel smiled at me. "Just going over my outline for class tomorrow, I can't wait to get back to school."

"Aren't you exhausted?"

"Yes I am but it is only seven o'clock and I really need to get this done."

I walked over and sat down on the bed next to her and slid myself backwards to rest my back against the headboard. I put my arm around her. "Your hair is still wet."

"Yes. It felt so good to take a hot shower." Alexander put his hand on my shoulder and touched the long scratch that Calicia had inflicted. "Who did this to you, was it Luke?"

I shook my head at him. "No, Calicia did it."

He touched my cheek next. "And your cheek, it is slightly swollen, was that Calcia also?"

"No, that was Luke." I heard a low growl expel from Alexander's throat. He was angry and I knew that he wanted to know everything that had happened to me while I had been held captive."

I looked at Ariel and was frantic with worry, what else hadn't she told me. I tried to contain my thoughts. "Why did he hit you?"

"It happened at my apartment when Luke and the others showed up. I tried to kick him in the jaw but my kick had no effect on him and then he hit me."

"Do you have any other cuts or bruises?"

"Just on my arm where he drew some blood."

"Yes, I saw the message he left on your apartment wall, Zack, Jeremy and Mia cleaned that up for me and re-painted. You wouldn't have wanted to see it. I was worried sick about you."

I looked directly into Alexander's face. "So that is why he took my blood. I am so sorry Alexander this is my fault. If I had listened to you none of this would have happened." Alexander had a peculiar look on his face and all of a sudden a thought struck me, what if he had changed his mind about us and wanted to break up?

"Alexander is everything ok?" He didn't answer me right away and I held my breath.

Alexander sighed. "Ariel you could have been killed. What happened just confirms what I feared about the danger of our relationship."

My heart almost stopped and I thought that he was going to break up with me. "Yes Alexander but I wasn't and everything is ok now."

Alexander cleared his throat. "I just don't know how to protect you twenty-four seven…."

I interrupted him before he could finish the sentence in which I thought he was going to break up with me. "You don't have to protect me Alexander."

Alexander raised his voice slightly. "Yes I do Ariel. What would you say if I asked you to move into the house with me and Antoinette?"

He took me completely by surprise. I thought he was going to break up with me. I sucked in a breath and then laughed.

"Are you ok Ariel?"

I smiled at him. "Yes, I am sorry, you just surprised me. I actually thought that you were trying to break up with me."

"No Ariel, I don't think that I could ever do that, even if I wanted to I think it is biologically impossible. But if you moved in here you would be a lot safer."

I laughed at Alexander's comment and I knew that my life would never be the same again but I didn't care, Alexander was my life now.

"You don't have to answer me right now if you don't want to? But it is the only way that I can think of to keep you safe. It is a much better idea than what Antoinette had."

"What was Antoinette's idea?"

"She thinks that you would be safer if you were a vampire."

"She thinks that you should change me?"

Alexander put his head down. "Yes."

"What do you think about that Alexander?"

He looked back up at me. "I guess we never really talked about a long term future."

"No we haven't, I mean I am aging and you are not. Your work is important to you and I would imagine that it will take a long time to change a lot of vampires back to humans."

Alexander nodded his head. "Yes Ariel it will."

"Alexander, you didn't answer my question, what do you think about changing me?"

"I don't want to think about it. I love you as you are?"

"Good because I love being human and I don't want to be a vampire."

He smiled at me. "Then it is settled but you didn't answer my question, what do you think about moving in?"

I knew that he was worried. "I would definitely be safer here with you and Antoinette, but will Antoinette mind? I am guessing that she is pretty mad at me right now?"

Alexander laughed. "She is not mad at you she is just concerned about everything."

"Do you mean about us?"

"Yes and about our work."

"I never asked you before - does Antoinette disapprove of us being together because I am human?"

I shook my head at Ariel. "No, it is not just that, it goes deeper than that for Antoinette."

"What do you mean?"

I knew that my sister would be angry at what I was about to tell Ariel but I felt that it was necessary. "Antoinette was in love with a human once herself"

I interrupted Alexander. "Oh, I would have never guessed that."

"Yes, it was during the fifteenth-century and his name was Kayal. He was my best friend and her mate."

"What happened to him?"

"He was killed because he helped to hide us from vampire hunters."

Ariel lowered her eyes. "I am sorry."

"Don't tell Antoinette that I told you about him, ok. She blames herself for his death."

Ariel looked up at me. "I won't."

I smiled at her. "Ariel, you never answered my question, about moving in with us?"

"Alright Alexander I will do it".

"Great. We can move all of your things out of your apartment this week, with the help of Zack, Jeremy and Mia it won't take us long."

"I will have to get a storage bin?"

I laughed at her. "Ariel, you don't need a storage bin this house has more empty bedrooms than a hotel. It is more than adequate to store your furniture."

"Alexander there is still something else that we need to talk about?"

"What is it?"

"I need to know more about you - I mean about vampires."

"Yes, Ariel you are right, but let's wait until after you get moved in to the house and then we will sit down and talk."

"Ok Alexander, if that is what you want." Alexander still looked worried and I didn't know exactly what to say to him to comfort him so I just said the first thing that popped into my head. "Look Alexander, I know you love me and you are worried about me, but I really am ok."

Alexander shook his head at me. "How can you say that, you were just abducted and taken to a house with thirty vampires. I just can't forget that. If anything had happened to you I just couldn't bear it."

I smiled and put my arms around his neck. "Relax, Alexander and have a little faith in love."

CHAPTER 9
NEW SEMESTER CLASS MEETS

I stood next to Alexander as he unlocked our class-room door. It was the first day of the new semester of Vampires 201, The Anatomy and Morphology of the Vampire, Part 2. Our Vampires 200 class had ended and Mirka, Lauren and Joseph had successfully handled the class while we were gone. Alexander opened the door and walked into the classroom and I followed him.

Alexander turned to face me. "Antoinette it feels so good to be back at school."

I smiled at him. "Yes it does. Oh! I forgot to tell you that I called Mirka last night and she said that everything went fine, but Principle Hines did come looking for us."

Alexander shook his head. "Imagine that, he has never come to our classroom before but does so when we are gone."

I laughed. "Yes. We should meet with him today to see what he wanted and to apologize to him for not getting back to him sooner."

Just then the bell rang. "Alexander, why don't you start out with the students today?"

"Ok, Antoinette, no problem."

I turned and walked away from Alexander and over to my desk and sat down. I watched while the students entered the classroom and then began taking their seats. Once they had all arrived and were seated I noticed that there were no vampire students in this class and I felt disappointed.

Alexander walked to the center of the room and addressed the students. "Good morning class and welcome to Part 2 of The Anatomy and Morphology of the Vampire. My name is Dr. Alexander Von-Allenberg and I would like to introduce my co-teacher and sister Dr. Antoinette Von-Allenberg. Both Antoinette and I are Professors in our fields of science and teaching, so you may address us in several different ways, by Professor, by Mr. or Ms. Von-Allenberg or simply by Alexander or Antoinette, we will leave that up to you individually. Class will meet daily for eight weeks." I turned and walked to the black board and scribbled the title of class across the board.

The Anatomy and Morphology of the Vampire Part II

When I turned back around I noticed Mirka, Joseph and Lauren sitting in the front row of the classroom. I smiled at them. "Welcome back Mirka, Joseph and Lauren."

Mirka smiled. "Thank you Alexander."

"Just for your information, next semester we will teach a class called, "Vampires 202, The Immortals." The class will be about some of the ancient cultures that drank blood and sought immortality. I would like to go around the room and let each of you introduce yourselves. Let's start with this row." I pointed to the first student in the first row.

The students began introducing their selves, "I am Mirka," "Joseph," "I'm Lauren," "I am Erin," "David," "Miles," "I am Nina," "Emily," "Jared," "Melanie," "Marcy," "Brian," "I am Adeline."

I noticed that there were no vampire students in our class. "All right then, I want to start with a recap from last semester's class Vampires 200. In that class we discussed how a vampire is very much alive, like a human but that a vampire's brain functions far exceed that of a human." Two male students laughed out loud, Erin and David. I looked at them.

Erin looked at me. "Sorry," he said.

I nodded my head at him. "That is alright remember this is a mythology class. As I was saying the vampire's brain functions exceed that of a human and the five senses known to mankind sight, hearing, taste, touch, and smell are extremely heightened in the vampire. The vampire brain differs from the human brain in that the human brain feeds off blood that circulates in the body, a vampire does not have an active vein system so the brain is fed by fresh human blood that is ingested - ingested is the key word here."

I looked at the students face's and saw that they looked confused. "Please keep in mind this is a mythology class and not a science class. A vampire can smell blood from a long distance away as well as hear sounds at least a mile away. Are there any questions so far?" No hands went up.

I watched Alexander while he taught class and I sensed that his heart just wasn't in his work today. I suspected that he was worried about Ariel being back at school and being in her classroom by herself, unprotected. I got up and walked to the center of the room and stood next to him and smiled at him.

When Antoinette looked over at me I could see from the look on her face that she wanted to take over class and I nodded my head at her. "Ok class, Antoinette would like to share some information with you."

I walked to my desk and sat down and Antoinette took control of our class.

"Hello class, as Alexander stated earlier you may address me however you feel most comfortable, Ms. Von-Allenberg, Professor or Antoinette and this is most definitely a mythology class, so please just take it for what it is. We do not give tests or quizzes in this class." I heard a sigh of relief from the students. "This class is meant to introduce and stimulate your interest in several different fields of study." I saw a hand go up it was Melanie, "Yes Melanie?"

Melanie lowered her hand. "What fields of study are you talking about?"

"Well, for example, Science, or Archeology." I saw a hand go up it was Miles, "Yes Miles?"

Miles put his hand down. "How does a vampire relate to Archeology?"

"That is a good question Miles. There have actually been many vampire-like corpses found over the years by Archeologists and Scientists."

His eyes widened. "Seriously, that is amazing."

"Yes, and as I said the class is meant to stimulate your interest in science in general. Alexander and I have traveled all over the world and participated in a large number of archeological digs, as a matter of fact when I finish lecturing Alexander and I have a specimen that we would like to show you from one of our digs."

Melanie raised her hand.

"Yes, Melanie?"

Melanie put her hand down. "What is it?" she asked.

I smiled at her. "It is a surprise so you will have to wait. Ok let's continue, now contrary to popular belief that vampires do not have blood in their bodies they actually do. They retain a small amount of blood, especially after feeding and it is slowly digested by the brain. When a human is infected with vampirism, one of the first things to shut down is the vein system and the body also stops producing blood and starts craving it. When this occurs, the secondary system used to circulate blood and fluids, takes over, this is the lymphatic system." I saw a hand go up, it was Erin again, "Yes Erin."

Erin put his hand down. "I am sorry I am really confused. I know that this is a mythology class but it really sounds like you and Professor Von-Allenberg believe in vampires."

I smiled at him. "Yes, you are correct we do." I saw a look of shock on Erin's face. Another hand went up. It was Brian, "Yes Brian?"

Brian put his hand down. "Ms. Von-Allenberg. What is the lymphatic system?"

"That is a really good question. The lymphatic system is like one big vein that goes around the whole human body without a break from head to toe and it carries fluids that feed the body tissues."

"Wow, that's amazing."

"Yes, that is how a vampire's body feeds the brain after the vein system shuts down. When a vampire drinks blood it enters the stomach and is absorbed from the colon tissue then enters the lymphatic system." I saw Erin's hand go up again. "Yes, Erin."

Erin lowered his hand. "I am surprised that you and Professor Von-Allenberg believe in vampires."

I smiled at him. "Why is that Erin?"

"Well, because you both are so educated. How can you believe in vampires?"

"Erin, there is a lot of documentation out there, I mean in books, in articles and on the internet about vampires. It is very interesting reading."

"Yes, but that's all made up like the movies."

"Are you sure?"

Erin smiled. "Of course it is made up...I mean there is no real evidence that vampires exist."

I laughed. "Well I disagree with you. You did not take our Vampires 101 class. In that class we talked about some of the corpses that have been found over the years, corpses with elongated teeth and claw-like nails, things indicative of a vampire."

Erin laughed. "I don't think they really found that stuff it is probably all faked."

I thought that now would be a good time to show the students the specimen that Alexander and I had brought to class. "Ok Erin that is certainly one possibility but I can assure you that the archeological digs that Alexander and I have participated in were valid digs and the specimens that we have found are quite genuine. As a matter of fact, we have brought such a specimen to class today for you all to look at." Every set of eyes in class was on me. I had their full attention.

Erin called out. "What did you bring?"

I glanced back at Alexander while he sat at his desk. He had been working on his medical papers. "Alexander, do you want to do the honors?"

Alexander looked up at me and smiled, "Of course, Antoinette."

I watched as Alexander opened his desk drawer and took out a glass jar marked "Specimen." He walked to the center of the room and stood next to me and held the jar up so that the students could see it. Alexander addressed the class.

"Alright, I am going to walk down each row and let you look at it. This is part of a jaw bone and some teeth from a vampire." I walked down the first row and heard a lot of low whisper's and comments going back and forth between the students. "This find is very, very old and dates from around the seventeenth century." I made my way down the second row. "When I finish showing it to you I will set it on my desk and you can get up from your seats and look at it, but don't pick the jar up." I made my way down the third and fourth row and then walked over to my desk and sat the jar on my desk. The students quickly got up from their seats and then gathered around my desk to look at the jar. They stood staring at it. "As I said, the specimen is from the seventeenth-century and Antoinette and I found it on a recent dig, so I assure you it is real."

Mirka looked astounded. "I can't believe it. I have never seen anything like this before."

"Yes Mirka it is a wonderful find."

Miles touched the jar with his finger. "This is amazing. Are there more specimens like this?"

"Yes Miles, lots of them."

He looked at me and his eyes widened. "Where are they Mr. Von-Allenberg? I have never seen anything like this in a museum."

I smiled at him. "You probably won't. These types of specimens are collected by collectors. Also not too many museums want to display things that they can't explain."

"How come this was never on the news or on television?" Joseph asked.

I turned my head toward Joseph. "This isn't the kind of stuff that would make the evening news Joseph and a lot of people would argue that is was just one of those bizarre things were someone had abnormal teeth."

The students all laughed. "Oh, I see what you mean," Joseph said.

"Yes, people tend to believe in what they want."

"Can we open the jar and touch it?" Erin asked.

I could tell that Erin still doubted the authenticity of the specimen. "Sure." I picked up the jar and took the lid off and tilted the jar toward Erin. "Go ahead and touch it."

"What is that white stuff in the jar?" Erin asked.

"It is a preservative for the bone, it won't hurt you."

Erin put his hand into the jar and touched the specimen. "It feels like bone."

I laughed. "It is bone and real teeth."

Erin looked confused. "How is this possible?"

The bell rang and Erin removed his hand from the jar and I put the lid back on it. "Ok class we will see you tomorrow." I watched as the students left the classroom.

Antoinette walked up and stood along side me. "That was fun Alexander, did you see the look on their faces."

"Yes."

I could tell that Alexander was still distracted and I assumed that he was worried about Ariel. "Alexander, are you ready to take a break and go to the teacher's lounge?" I watched his face light up. I knew that Ariel would probably be in the teacher's lounge during break and that he wanted to see her.

Alexander smiled at me. "Yes, let's go."

Alexander led the way to the door and I followed. He walked out of the classroom and I stopped at the door and turned off the lights and pulled the door tightly closed. We walked out of our building and across the grass to the main building. The teacher's lounge was on the first floor. We entered the building and we were greeted by Principle Hines secretary, Mrs. Teaple. I often wondered if she had a thing for Alexander.

Her face beamed at his presence. "Hello Alexander and Antoinette."

Alexander smiled at her. "Hello Mrs. Teaple how are you doing today?"

She smiled in return. "Just fine Alexander and you?"

"I am doing great, thanks."

I followed Alexander down the hall and through the door of the teacher's lounge. As soon as we entered it I saw Ariel, she sat at a small table all by herself. I turned my head to my brother. "I am going to go and check our mailbox and then sit over at that table," I said and pointed to table near Ariel's.

"Ok Antoinette I am going to go over and talk to her for a moment." I walked away from Antoinette and over to Ariel's table and sat down.

Ariel looked at me. "Hi Alexander, how is your day going?"

"Great, it feels good to be back at work."

She smiled. "Yes it does, I missed my classroom and my students."

"Ariel did you notice anything abnormal today?"

"No Alexander – nothing out of the ordinary. I promised you that I would tell you right away if anything happens. I am being very careful I learned my lesson."

I nodded my head at her. "Good."

"Alexander have you seen Principle Hines yet?"

"No why?"

"Because he caught me earlier in the hallway to welcome me back and asked me to remind you and Antoinette that he needs to talk to you."

"Yes, we know he is looking for us. We are going to see him when we leave here." The bell rang and I stood up. "Ariel, I will see you after school in the parking lot, bye."

"Bye Alexander."

I left Ariel in the teacher's lounge and Antoinette got up from the table she sat at and followed me out into the hallway. I turned to face her. "Should we go and see Principle Hines now?"

"Yes, what are you going to tell him if he asks why we weren't in class?"

I shook my head at her. "I am not sure but I will think of something."

I followed Alexander down the hall and he stopped at Mrs. Teaple's desk. "Hello again Mrs. Teaple I believe that Principle Hines wants to see Antoinette and I?"

She smiled broadly at him. "Yes Alexander he is expecting you, go right in." I left Mrs. Teaple's desk and walked over to Principle Hines door and Antoinette followed me. I stopped at the door and knocked.

I heard him call out. "Come in."

I opened the door and stepped in. "Hello Sir, I understand that you have been looking for us. Is this a good time?"

"Yes Alexander. Please come in and take a seat."

I walked over and sat in one of the chairs that faced his desk and Antoinette followed behind me and then sat in another. "I am sorry that we missed you the other day when you came to class."

Principle Hines narrowed his eyes at me. "Yes, where were you?"

"We had a bit of an emergency and had to rush home."

Principle Hines looked curious. "Oh, really what happened?"

"The security alarm went off at our house and the security company that monitors it called us. We had a break in."

Principle Hines looked concerned. "In your neighborhood that is simply shocking."

I nodded my head at him. "Yes Sir, it is a very good neighborhood but nonetheless it happened."

"Is everything alright, was anything taken?"

"Everything is fine and no, nothing was taken, apparently the alarm frightened off the intruder." I didn't enjoy lying to him but it was necessary under the circumstances.

"Well thank goodness nothing was taken."

"Yes Sir, it makes the money spent on the system worth it. What did you want to talk to us about?"

"Oh yes, back to that. It is about homecoming and the football game this Friday night. We are having a pep rally Thursday afternoon and I need two volunteers. I was hoping that you an Antoinette would volunteer to help with it?"

I smiled at him. "Absolutely Sir, what is it that you would you like us to do?"

"Well I need you to steer the kids into the gym for the rally and then just stand by the doors and watch them. I have had a problem with kids sneaking out and cutting school during these rallies"

"Sure, we can do that. We will keep a close eye on them."

Principle Hines smiled. "Thank you both. I also wanted to tell you both that I appreciate the support that you are giving the school. I haven't had the chance to tell you this but I am very pleased with your performance. Your class seems to be quite popular and my offices attendants tell me that it fills quicker than any of the others."

"Thank you Sir?"

Principle Hines turned his head to Antoinette. "Antoinette you have been exceedingly quite is there anything that you would like to add to the conversation."

"No Sir, other than thank you for that lovely compliment. Both Alexander and I are very happy with our jobs here."

"I am most glad to hear that," Principle Hines said and then stood up from his chair. "Thank you for coming in to see me."

I stood up from my chair and then Antoinette stood up from her chair and we walked to the door and left his office.

CHAPTER 10
ANREE THE VAMPIRE

Luke had taken all my money, twenty-five of my vampires were dead and my coven burned to the ground. I concluded that Luke had planned the whole thing, I had underestimated him and it wouldn't happen again. I had no alternative but to seek the help of an old friend, Anree. It was a long trip to France and it took me a while to locate him but I finally found him living quite well, in the south of France. I paused and stared at the ten foot iron gates that surrounded his mansion. It sat back from the road and was hid by the trees and heavy shrubbery. I knew that the moment I leapt over the gates I would probably be surrounded by vampires from Anree's coven and I was right. Immediately after my jump over the gates two vampires instantly appeared. I spoke quickly to them. "I am an old friend of Anree's and he will want to see me."

The short vampire with brown hair and eyes spoke. "We will see about that. What is your name?"

"Calicia Claig," I told them. They escorted me through the trees and up to the mansion and then onto the veranda and through the doors and then inside. We walked down a long marble floored hallway and then into a huge living room where I saw Anree sitting on a Victorian couch.

He turned his head to me and looked absolutely shocked to see me. "Calicia, moi cheri (my dear)."

"Yes Anree it has been a very long time. You are looking well."

He stood to greet me. He was the same height as me, five-foot nine inches tall and had brown hair and brown eyes.

He walked over to me. "Ah! Cheri (sweetheart), you are just as beautiful as ever. What business do you have in France?"

I batted my eyelashes at him. "You ask me that, after all that we've shared? Why I have come to see you Anree." I could tell by the look on his face that he didn't believe me.

He laughed and then kissed me on the cheek. "Oui (Yes) I have not seen you in a hundred years, not one visit, or a phone call. I know you too well, you want something cheri (sweetheart), what is it?"

I smiled at him. "Anree is that anyway to talk to an old love."

"Oui (Yes) Calicia Claig's coven has fallen and she needs my help."

I momentarily turned my face away from him and then turned it back. "So you have heard then?"

"Oui (Yes)."

"How did you find out?"

Anree laughed. "That step son of yours, Luke. He has told half the vampire community what he did to you."

I could feel my own muscles tighten in anger. "That figures," I said and flicked at a fly in the air as it passed by me and sliced it in two.

Anree smiled. "Oui (Yes) it appears that you should have married me and not Luke's father, the old man, what was his name, I believe it was Earl?"

I remained silent.

His eyes narrowed. "Why should I help you now?"

I stepped closer to Anree. "Oh, I don't know, for old time sake. You once told me that you loved me."

"Oui (Yes), I did tell you that."

I smiled at him. "Anree I have a proposal for you."

He laughed. "Oh, now you propose to me. I have waited a century to hear you say those words Calicia."

I shook my head at him. "Knock it off Anree I am talking about a business proposal you fool."

"And I am talking about a marriage proposal Calicia. If you want my help it will cost you."

His offer shocked me. "You can't be serious?"

He nodded his head at me. "Oh, but I am moi cheri (my dear) I hear wedding bells or you will get no help from me."

"This is extortion! You know I don't really love you, not that way."

"Since when do you care about love Calicia? I have loved you since we first met, before you married that fool Earl, you chose poorly."

I glared at him. "I chose what met my purpose."

"Ah, oui (yes) you did and Earl met an untimely death after your marriage and you took over his coven. Tell me Calicia does Luke know that you killed his father?"

I momentarily looked away from him and then turned my head back to him. "I don't know what you are talking about. Earl was killed by a rival coven."

Anree laughed. "You can lie to Luke, but not to me. That rival coven you speak of, some of the members now belong to my coven. Oh sure, you tried to cover your tracks and you thought you killed off everyone that had helped you but a few of them got away, remember?"

"Yes, I remember."

"So tell me again why I should help you?"

I knew my ruse was useless. "Luke attacked my coven and stole all of my money and jewels."

"How much did he get?"

"He got everything, twenty million dollars and millions in jewelry and jewels. It took me years to amass those amounts. You are a powerful vampire now Anree with a large coven, you can help me."

"Perhaps Luke found out that you had his father killed?"

"I hadn't considered that possibility but how would he have found out, surely you didn't tell him, did you?"

"Why would I do that moi cheri (my love)?"

"Help me Anree, I always regretted marrying Earl, I should have married you." I smiled at him but could tell by the look in his eyes that he wasn't buying it.

Anree narrowed his eyes at me. "Calicia tell me the real reason that Luke and the others attacked your coven?"

I realized that I would have to tell him the truth. "Anree have you heard about the two doctors, from England, the ones that some of the covens are looking for?"

Anree looked surprised. "Yes, I have why?"

"Because I met them, they were at my coven and they helped Luke to destroy it."

Anree laughed loudly. "Why doesn't that surprise me Calicia that you would have something to do with them."

"Anree listen to me, they have a medicine that makes vampires sleep. It is priceless just think of the possibilities that we could encompass together, taking over coven after coven and eliminating covens. We could rule the vampire world!"

Anree's eyes lit up. "Now, that is the Calicia Claig that I remember and love. Yes it appears that we do have a lot to discuss after all, but my business proposal still stands."

I looked at him. "Yes Anree."

"Good Calicia, then we leave for America at once!"

CHAPTER 11
CLASS MEETS AGAIN

I stood at the door of our classroom and Antoinette stood behind me. I unlocked the door and opened it and we walked inside and stood near the door. The bell rang.

Antoinette looked over at me. "Here come the students".

I smiled at her. I watched as the students walked in together in one's and two's and took their seats. I felt disappointed that there were no vampire students in our class but I knew that it would be a quiet semester and we could use the time to re-think and re-organize our situation. Calicia and Luke were alive and still out there somewhere and I knew that Calicia was not the forgiving type. I mean we destroyed her entire coven and it takes a vampire a long time to build up a trustworthy coven, they become family in the process. The students had taken their seats.

Antoinette looked back at me. "Alexander would you like me to start off this morning?"

I nodded my head at her. "Sure, thanks." I turned and walked over to my desk and sat down. I really needed to continue work on my research. This was the last piece of the DNA puzzle for the vampire-human anatomy relationship that I hadn't quite worked out yet. It was the genetic sequencing for the half vampire, half human child, and as of yet I was unable to change such a child back to a human. I hoped to resolve this issue soon.

My brother sat at his desk and I moved to the center of the room. "Good morning class." I heard a mixture of replies, good morning Antoinette, Ms. Von-Allenberg and Professor. I was excited because I knew that today the students would find class particularly interesting. "Alright class let's get started, I think that you are going to enjoy our discussion today. We are going to talk about the fiction of television and how vampires are portrayed on television and compare that to the reality of a vampire. You may reference any shows or movies that you have seen and ask any questions that you like about vampires. Who would like to start?" I saw a hand go up, it was Jared. "Yes, Jared."

Jared lowered his hand. "I have seen some movies about vampires. In the movies they are very strong, why is that?"

I smiled at him. "That is a good question. When a human changes to a vampire their bones harden and calcify and double in thickness, this makes them quite strong, much stronger than humans. But I must say that their strength is exaggerated a bit in the movies. They are actually about three times stronger than a human." I saw another hand go up, it was Nina. "Yes Nina?"

Nina put her hand down. "How do you know this?"

"Well, some of the vampire-like bodies that we have exhumed were studied in labs and the bone was tested for strength."

Nina looked amazed. "Wow! I have another question, in the movies to become a vampire you have to be bitten by a vampire is that true? I mean mythically speaking."

"Yes." I saw another hand up, it was Brian. "Yes Brian."

Brian put his hand down. "How can someone become a vampire from just a bite? I mean in some movies that I have seen they talk about venom that vampires inject into their victim. Is that true?"

I laughed quite loudly. "No, that is absolutely not true. A vampires teeth are quite the same as a human's except for the fangs that extract and re-tract when they feed. What actually happens is that when the victim is bitten, it is usually a deep bite and the saliva from the vampire infects the human much like an animal bite. It is similar to a rabbit animal that carries the rabies virus." I watched the intrigue on my students faces.

Brian's eyes widened. "That's amazing," he said.

I saw another hand go up, it was Melanie. "Yes, Melanie."

Melanie lowered her hand. "Ms. Von-Allenberg you said that you and Alexander believe that vampires did exist and you showed us that specimen of the jaw bone and teeth, so if vampires were infected with a virus like you just said, then why can't they be cured?"

Melanie's question totally caught me off guard and Alexander jumped from his desk and moved to my side. "If you don't mind Antoinette I will take this question?"

I glanced at him and smiled. I was glad that Alexander had reacted as he did because I didn't have an answer prepared for Melanie's question.

Alexander spoke. "Well Melanie that is a question that we couldn't possibly answer at this time. The vampire-like bodies that have been exhumed were all severely – desecrated. The tissue samples taken by archeologist teams yielded nothing about viruses despite the physical abnormalities of the vampire-like corpses, like the elongated teeth and claws. So at this point the virus is just a theory."

Melanie looked confused. "What do you mean by severely desecrated corpses?"

"Well, we covered a lot of this information in our Vampires 101 class, but I guess now would be a good time to go over some of it. Most of the vampire-like bodies found had their heads severed and in some cases their hands or feet cut off. There was a body found that dates from the sixteenth-century, of a female who had not only been staked through the heart but had a huge brick stuffed in the mouth, against the fangs."

Melanie looked shocked. "Why was a brick stuffed in the mouth?"

"We are not sure Melanie, but our speculation is that it was meant to keep the jaw from retracting, back to its human form, like to be trapped in the vampire state after they had staked the heart as proof that she really was indeed a vampire."

She smiled. "This stuff is just amazing."

"Yes it is." I saw another hand go up, it was Emily. "If you all don't mind I will let Antoinette get back to answering your questions." I walked back to my desk and sat down and continued my work on my medical papers while Antoinette addressed the class.

"What is your question Emily?"

Emily lowered her hand. "Ms. Von-Allenberg I was wondering about vampire children like in the movies. Can a vampire have children?"

I looked at Emily. Alexander and I were getting some very intriguing questions and in one way it pleased me because it meant that the students were curious and taking the subject matter seriously but on the other hand some of the questions weren't expected and I was unprepared to answer them. I smiled at Emily. "Emily, again this would be speculation on our part but as Alexander said it is difficult to get accurate genetic information from desecrated corpses, but here goes. What we do know comes from some of the myths from different cultures from all over the world. There are myths that stem from the deepest jungles of the world all the way to Australia about half vampire and half human children. What Alexander and I suspect is that only the male vampire is fertile meaning that, the mother would have to be human." I paused briefly because I was not sure how much more information Alexander would want me to disclose about this subject. He was currently doing research on this very topic. I looked over at my brother for his ok.

He nodded his head at me. "Please continue Antoinette."

I smiled at him and then turned back to Emily. "Alright then, as I was saying we suspect that the mother would have to be human in order to conceive and carry the half vampire, half human child but that the birth would be very difficult, if not impossible for a human."

Emily looked very interested. "What do you mean?"

"Well, a vampire child would be quite strong and a human mother probably wouldn't survive the birth. It is quite possible that the child might just claw its way out during birth." I could see that I had surprised some of the students with my answer.

"Oh, well couldn't they do a C-section?"

I realized that this subject was becoming a little too involved for basic anatomy so I decided to put an end to the discussion, "My answer would only be speculation at this point. I do know however, that C-sections weren't performed that many years ago."

"Ok Ms. Von-Allenberg."

I saw another hand go up, it was Miles. "Yes Miles?"

Miles put his hand down. "In some of the movies that I have seen after someone has been bitten by a vampire they can get a transfusion to cure them."

I laughed. "If it were only that easy," I thought to myself. "No I don't think that would really work Miles." I saw another hand go up, "Yes Melanie?"

Melanie put her hand down. "What about sucking the venom out? I saw that in a movie."

"No, that wouldn't work either. Once a vampire bites you I am afraid there is nothing you can do to stop from turning into one? Are there any more questions? No one else raised their hands. "Ok, I will do a bit of a recap from last semester. Last semester we talked about a vampire's heart and how on television vampires do not have a heart beat, this is not true. A vampire's heart still beats but it is such a faint beat that it is undetected by modern machinery. Even though it does beat it is not strong enough to circulate blood throughout the body so the vampire's muscle system takes over and serves as an internal pump to push the blood through the lymphatic system to feed the brain. A vampire's anatomy isn't all that different from a human." I saw a hand go up, it was Brian. "Yes Brian."

Brian put his hand down. "What about the other organs?"

"Only the brain, heart, lungs, stomach and lymphatic system functions in order to keep a vampire alive. The rest of the organs, the kidney's, bladder, liver, pancreas, gallbladder and other organs shut down."

"So the other organs just die?"

"No Brian, they don't die, they just lay dormant, like they are asleep."

"Anymore questions?" No one raised their hand. "Ok more of a recap from last semester. Alexander and I believe that vampires first surfaced during the eleventh-century. Between the eleventh-century and the four-teenth-century little was known about vampires and they kept an extremely low profile. During the four-teenth-century, after Columbus discovered America is when vampires started coming to America. The four-teenth-century was called the "Age of Enlightenment." This was when humans actively started hunting vampires and when books were first written on how to hunt vam-pires. This was also the time when "Vlad Dracula" or "Vlad the Impaler" was born, some of you may have heard of him. Between the fourteenth-century and the seventeenth-century vampires – gained publicity and popularity, in the seventeenth-century the first modern vampire poem was written, "Der Vampire." After the Salem Witch Trials, the New England vampire panic occurred and vampires ran ramped on the East Coast, they spread out all over the world and started their own covens. In the country of Bulgaria there are over one-hundred cases of vampire-like bodies that have been discovered that date back to the fifteenth-century, these bodies had iron stakes driven through the hearts. Bodies like these were the result of vampire hunts that were active back then. A more recent case is of some children who were playing in a field. They discovered a gravesite that dates from the sixteenth-century and the graves were typical burials from that period. The archeological team found some rocks on top of a coffin and the rocks were used as some type of identifier for the coffin. It contained a body that had been dismembered. The bones were taken to a lab for analysis and determined that the breaks and fractures occurred after the victim had died. Do you have any questions so far?" No one raised their hand. "Ok then I have a small assignment for you it is titled, "If I were a vampire?" I want you to write a paragraph or two about what you would do if you were a vampire and the next time that we meet we will discuss your papers." The bell rang and the students got up from their desks and left the classroom.

Alexander got up from his desk and walked to my side. I turned my head to him. "So how is your research going?"

"I am getting closer Antoinette, the DNA sequencing that I have worked out is really starting to make sense."

I smiled at him. "That is great Alexander. The last piece of the DNA puzzle that we need in order to change the half vampire, half human children, back to humans. Our work is almost complete!"

CHAPTER 12
THE PEP RALLY

I stood at one of the gym doors and Alexander stood at another. Principle Hines had asked us to volunteer to watch the doors during the rally to ensure that students did not sneak out of the gym. The gym was packed full of students, they filled the wooden bleachers and lined the walls. Principle Hines stood in the center of the gym at the podium and was surrounded by several faculty members that included Ariel and some members of the football team. I assumed that Ariel would be speaking at some point. I watched as Principle Hines walked up to the podium and flicked the microphone with his finger.

He spoke with enthusiasm and threw his arms up into the air. "Hello Lincoln High are you all pumped about the big game against Washington High?"

The students yelled out loudly and cheered.

Principle Hines continued, "We took a beating from them two years in a row but this year we have a heck of

a football team and I know that we are going to be vic-
torious."

I smiled. These were the simple things in life that I felt
were important for kids. Alexander and I did not have
memories like this, there were no schools in our village
and we were home schooled. After we were changed and
when modern medicine and technology progressed we
had to repeat college and medical school over and over
again to keep current with human anatomy. We never
had fun academically and that was why we wanted to
become teachers. I listened as Principle Hines continued
to motivate the students.

"I have a bet going with Principle Miller over at
Washington High and the loosing team's Principle will
have to wear a t-shirt to school for a whole week that
says, "Looser." You wouldn't want me to have to wear
that t-shirt, would you?"

The students yelled out loudly a variety of responses,
"No way Principle Hines," "Won't happen," and "We
will beat them black and blue."

Principle Hines stepped away from the podium and
Coach Looms stepped up to it. "Hello, Lincoln High, let
me hear a big hello out there!"

The student's voices roared through the gym. I
looked across the gym and saw Alexander standing at

the door across from me. He was staring at Ariel as she stood near the podium with the other teachers.

Coach Looms continued to speak. "As Principle Hines said we have an awesome football team this year. These guys are pumped and ready to take on Washington High. They have trained and worked hard for this game and they are going to pulverize them!"

I heard more cheering and yelling amongst the students. Coach Looms continued on, "I would like to introduce the captain of our team, Erin Lampbert and our leading defensive line man, David Walburn."

Erin and David stepped away from the small group of football players that they had stood with and walked up to the podium. Erin positioned him self at the podium and David stood next to him.

Erin spoke. "Most of you know me I am Erin Lampbert, captain and quarter back of our football team and this is David Walburn our leading defensive line man and I just want to say a few words, The Lions rock! This year our player's are giving the word "Jocks" a whole new meaning, we are pumped and ready for action and Washington High won't know what hit them."

The students cheered loudly. Principle Hines stepped back up to the podium and Erin and David walked back to the group and stood with them.

Principle Hines spoke. "And now on a more serious note Ms. Ariel Domande, our Greek Mythology teacher would like to talk to you for a moment about game night."

I watched while Ariel walked up to the podium, her five-foot-two inch frame was barely visible behind it as she prepared herself to speak. "Hello Lincoln High, I am Ms. Domande and I am on the refreshments committee for game night. I want to inform you that refreshments will be served after the game, here in the gymnasium and as we are predicting it will be a victory celebration."

All of the students cheered and Ariel continued. "Now on a more serious note I have to talk to you about a few do's and don'ts during game night. All of the entry points to the bleachers at the playing field will be clearly marked, as enter and exit. Please use only these points of entry or exit, we do not want students roaming around school grounds at night during the game. There are some areas on school grounds, like storage facilities that are clearly marked, "Do not enter." It is for your own safety that you follow the rules. We are strictly enforcing the "No alcohol" rule on school grounds and I just want to make it clear that we will have a zero tolerance for it. Principle Hines has asked me to inform you that anyone caught with alcohol or who is intoxicated on school grounds will be suspended indefinitely for the remainder of the school year. That translates to, "You will find another school to attend," I hope this is clear. We will never have a repeat of the horrible accident that occurred last semester." I didn't want to elaborate on the subject of Melissa and Levi's death so I just left it at that. "Thank you for your atten-tion." I left the podium and instead of returning to the group of faculty I walked toward the door to get a drink of water. As I neared the door I saw Antoinette standing guard at it. "Hello Antoinette."

"Hi Ariel, are you leaving now?"

"Oh no, I am just stepping out into the hall to get a drink of water, I will be right back." I walked out of the door of the gym and down the hallway to the drinking fountain and bent over and took a drink of water. As I straightened my body up and turned around I saw Luke standing there. "Luke?"

"Hello Ariel, I just wanted to see you again and apol-ogize for hitting you and for what I did, I mean kidnap-ping you and taking you to Canada, to Calicia."

I shook my head at him. "Luke it really wasn't about me was it. It was about you stealing your step mother's money."

Luke put his head down momentarily and then raised it again. "It was like that but then it wasn't. I am truly sorry for hitting you. It is not something I am proud of."

"You apologized to me already at the cabin, remember? Didn't you mean it then?"

"Of course I did, but it wasn't really me then, it's complicated. I can't explain it to you so that you would understand. It didn't feel like me, but now it does. I just wanted to tell you again, that's all."

I stared at him. "I think I understand?"

"Do you? Do you really Ariel?" Luke reached out and brushed a strand of hair that had fallen against my cheek.

"Thank you, I hate it when my hair does that."

"You have lovely hair."

Something was different about him. It was as if he had become that southern gentleman that we were talking about that night, in the cabin when he was telling me about how he grew up in the south. "Is that what you came here for, to apologize to me?"

"No, that is not the only reason. I have a confession, when I took you that day, from your apartment...." Luke paused and put his head down and then lifted it back up and looked me in the eyes and continued speaking, "I was actually planning to change you but I couldn't."

"Why?"

Luke smiled. "Because you are perfect just as you are."

His remark surprised me. "Well thank you again for keeping me safe."

"Ariel, there is one more thing that you need to know."

"What is it?"

"That I have no intention of ever hurting you again. I want you to know that and I want you to believe me. The world is a much better place with you in it."

As quickly as I looked up and into Luke's blue eyes he had disappeared. I would never get used to how quickly vampires moved. I walked back into the pep rally and joined the group of faculty near the podium.

Principle Hines stood at the podium. "Alright, bring out the mascot."

The school mascot, a student dressed as a lion ran around the gym while a tape played roaring sounds in the background. Students threw streamers of black and blue ribbons, the opposing team's colors, the Washington Eagles around the gym and the lion shredded them as they fell to the floor.

Principle Hines spoke again. "Alright everyone, thank you for coming, you are dismissed and may return to your classrooms."

I left the group of faculty and hurried toward the gym doors where Antoinette stood. I deliberately avoided going to the other side of the gym where Alexander stood by the door. I needed to think, I was confused, I knew that I should tell Alexander and Antoinette that I had seen Luke, but I just couldn't. I analyzed the situation in my mind, Alexander was furious with Luke for his having hit me, Luke obviously meant me no harm if he had he would have attacked me in the hallway. He said that I had nothing to fear from him and I believed him. I didn't want anymore fighting but there was something else too that I just didn't understand, Luke seemed different to me now and I didn't know how to feel about that. I approached the door and saw Antoinette.

"Ariel, aren't you going to wait for Alexander?"

"No I really need to get back to my classroom, tell him I will see him after school."

"Ok, I will let him know." As Ariel walked past me and through the gym door I sensed that something was wrong.

CHAPTER 13
CLASS MEETS AGAIN

I stood just inside the classroom door and watched while our students entered and took their seats. Alexander had already seated himself at his desk and would be working on his medical papers. He had been devoting a lot of time to his research lately and I was glad. The bell rang and I walked to the center of the room. "Good morning everyone," I heard a mixture of replies, good morning Antoinette, Ms. Von-Allenberg and Professor. "Last time we met I gave you an assignment, I asked you to write a short paragraph or two about what you would do if you were a vampire. I am curious to hear what you have written. Would anyone like to volunteer to read their assignment?" It took a moment but then a few hands were raised. "Alright, Miles go ahead."

Miles put his hand down. "Well, if I were a vampire I would become a rock star and be really rich and famous and I would move to Los Angeles."

I smiled. "Thank you, Miles." I saw David's hand raised, "Yes David."

David lowered his hand and cleared his throat, "I would become a professional football player and be the best player in the NFL."

"Sounds like a good plan, thank you David." Jared had his hand raised, "Go ahead Jared."

Jared put his hand down. "If I were a vampire I would use some of my powers, like hearing or seeing to gain information on the stock market. I would invest money and make a lot of money and then buy a mansion and a couple of new cars and continue to invest money and never have to work again."

I laughed. "Alright, thank you Jared." Nina had her hand raised. "Nina, go ahead."

Nina put her hand down. "I think it would be cool to live forever. I would change the rest of my family and friends so that we could all live together, forever. I would get a big penthouse in New York City and shop all the time and maybe even, become a famous clothes designer."

"Thank you Nina, that sounds like a lot of fun. Shopping and clothes are my passions too, let's stay in touch." I saw Mirka's hand go up and I was curious to see what her idea of being a vampire would be. "Yes Mirka?"

Mirka put her hand down. "If I were a vampire I think that I would become a scientist or doctor and try and find a cure for vampires so that they could be human again."

Mirka's answer shocked me. "Thank you Mirka, that is very admirable." Melanie had her hand up, "Go ahead Melanie."

Melanie put her hand down. "If I were a vampire I would become a famous scientist and work for NASA and be the first vampire in space."

I was surprised at how many of my students had associated being a vampire with having a lot of money or being famous. "Thank you Melanie." No one else had their hand raised. "Ok it looks as if we are finished I am not going to force anyone to read the assignment. I was going to lecture to you but we don't have enough time for that so I will entertain a question or two about movies or books about vampires and any questions that you might have. I saw a hand go up it was Brian, "Yes, Brian?"

Brian lowered his hand. "I was going to ask this question during our last class but I didn't get a chance. In some movies that I have seen when a human changes into a vampire it shows them in a lot of pain, is that really true?"

I was glad that Brian had asked this question, no one had asked it before. "That is a very good question Brian, thank you for asking it. Let me first say that my answer will be based on medical evidence that Alexander and I have obtained from corpses that were exhumed and examined and on medical tests that were performed on tissues, bones and dried up organs. Alexander has also written several articles for archeological magazines regarding, vampires as a myth and the change process that occurs when changing from a human to a vampire, mythically speaking. I think that I will just paraphrase some of his work and relay that information to all of you, so here goes. We believe that after a human is infected with the virus it enters their blood stream and causes major changes in the human body. We believe that organs shut down and body functions shut down and that this process would be extremely painful." Brian had raised his hand again, "Yes, Brian."

Brian put his hand down. "In one movie that I saw when the human was changing to a vampire, he was burning hot and unconscious?"

I didn't want to give the students too much detail about the change process if I did I might loose their interest because what I was telling them was supposed to come from myth and not real life experience as I knew it. I continued on, "There is no evidence from the tissue samples that we studied of any process of heat that occurs during the change, it is quite the opposite. The human becomes exceptionally cold during the changing process as the organs shut down. The tissue and skin becomes cold, numb, waxy, shinny looking and very hard."

"Wow, Miss Von-Allenberg that is amazing. It sounds like you and Alexander have studied a lot about vampires."

"Yes, we have Brian. We have examined a lot of unusual corpses over the years and found many artifacts that relate to vampires from all over the world."

"So how long does it take for a human to change to a vampire?"

"We estimate that it takes between two and three days for the change process to be complete because that is usually how long organs take to shut down, but not all humans do survive the change?"

Brian's eyes widened. "How do you know that?"

"Because we have examined some bodies that we believe were bitten by a vampire, for example they had puncture marks in the neck or on an arm but the victim still had blood in their body and the wound was not sufficient to cause death but yet the change did not occur."

Brian looked confused. "So what does that mean?"

"It means that they died during the change process, for example they might have had a bad heart or had a heart attack or a brain aneurism or something biological happened that stopped the change and caused their heart to stop. If a human's heart stops beating before the change occurs, they will die." Just then the bell rang. "Alright class, see you next time." The students rose from their seats and began walking out of the classroom. Alexander remained seated at his desk and I walked over and stood alongside it. "We have a great bunch of students this semester."

Alexander looked up at me. "Yes, but no vampires."

"That is alright Alexander I think we need a break anyway. We need to re-organize and re-think some of our strategies. I mean things are happening faster than we anticipated."

"Yes, you are right about that Antoinette."

CHAPTER 14
THE FUTURE

I sat in my office in my medical clinic on the third floor of the house. I was deep in thought about what Antoinette and I had talked about yesterday, after our class had ended, about being better prepared for what the future might hold. We needed to make every effort possible to keep our work a secret and I knew that it would be difficult. My cell phone rang and interrupted my thoughts. I reached for it and clicked talk. "Hello?"

"Hello Alexander it is Charles, I got the message that you left me. I am glad that everything went well and that Ariel is safely home."

"Yes, Charles everything went well but there were some issues."

"What do you mean?"

"Well Luke, Darla, Matt and Jason got away as well as did Calicia Claig."

"What about her coven?"

"We completely destroyed it and then Luke burned the cabin down."

"Really, why would he do that?"

"Well it turns out that he had alternative plans of his own. He took all of Calcia's money and he killed some of her vampires before we got to them."

"Well it appears that he was working to your advantage so I wouldn't worry too much about him now. He may have what he wants, the money, I mean."

I hoped that Charles was right but somehow I had an agonizing feeling that Luke still had an interest in Ariel. "I hope you are right Charles but I am afraid that we haven't heard the last of Calicia Claig. After having met her I agree that she definitely lives up to her reputation of being ruthless."

"Yes, Alexander that is the reason that I am calling. I have been giving that a lot of thought and I think I have a solution to your problem."

"Charles, any ideas that you have are welcomed."

"Alexander, I think that Calicia will make contact with you sometime in the near future and when she does try and arrange a meeting with her."

"Why?"

"Because, you should meet with her and bring Mia along and demonstrate Mia's gift to Calicia, let her put a vampire to sleep and then concoct a story of how Luke intentionally spread rumors about how you have a medicine that makes vampires sleep. Insist that Mia is your weapon and that there is no vampire anesthesia."

"Charles, you are a genius. I know I have told you that before but I truly mean it. It is absolutely brilliant."

"Thank you Alexander, but it is you who are the real genius. You cured vampirism. Sometimes I still can't believe that I am human now."

"Thank you Charles."

"Oh, and just a reminder, Emma's wedding is only a few months away."

"We couldn't forget about it, we are looking forward to it, especially Antoinette. We consider you all family Charles."

"We consider you both our family also. I had better go, take care."

"You take care too Charles." I hung up the phone and sat at my desk for a moment. Charles had solved our problem, it was the perfect plan. I resumed my work.

* * *

Alexander was hard at work at his desk when I walked into the room and stood behind his chair. "Is Ariel in her room?"

"Yes, I left her just a while ago. I have been working on my research papers."

"How are they coming?"

"I am getting close Antoinette, very close."

"That's great Alexander, finally the last piece of the puzzle."

"Yes, if I can just work out this genetic sequencing. It is so much more complicated with the half vampire half human child because so much of their body functions as a human. It has been difficult for me to determine what organs are functioning and which are not. One mistake and it could prove fatal to the patient."

I smiled at my brother. "I know you will figure it out. In the meantime we still have Luke and Calicia Claig to worry about."

"Yes, I am sure that Luke will try and start another coven now that he has money and I expect to hear from him in the future."

"I agree but I expect to hear from Calicia Claig sooner than that."

"I think you are right Antoinette. Charles just called me a little while ago and he has the perfect solution to end our dealings with Calicia Claig."

"Really, what is that?"

"Charles feels that Calicia will contact us fairly soon. He suggested that when she does we are to meet with her."

"Why on earth would we want to do that?"

"So that we can introduce Calicia to Mia and demonstrate Mia's gift, her ability to put a vampire to sleep. Then we convince Calicia that there never was a vampire anesthesia or as she referred to it, – "A medicine that makes vampires sleep," we tell her that Luke lied to her just to trick her to steal her money."

I laughed out loud. "That is a brilliant idea."

"Yes sister, it is pure genius. I only wish that I had thought of it."

"You would have if you didn't have so many other things on your mind."

I looked over at my sister and knew that she was referring to Ariel. "You mean that I have Ariel on my mind don't you?"

I briefly turned my head away from my brother and then back to him. "Yes that is what I mean."

"Well I have my own solution for Ariel."

"What do you mean Alexander?" I watched as my brother opened his desk drawer and took out a small black velvet box. I recognized it instantly, it was our mother's and she must have sent it from England to

Alexander. He was going to propose to Ariel and he hadn't even told me about it. My eyes went from the ring box back to my brother's face.

"Yes sister aren't you going to congratulate me?"

I was speechless.

"Antoinette, do I have your blessing?"

My mind was racing a hundred miles an hour, marriage, love, the confusion, the complications – the trauma. I allowed my mind to wander back to Kayal, my love, he had once proposed to me.

"Antonette?"

I smiled at him. "I am sorry Alexander. Yes of course, it makes sense, it is the only way you can protect her, I mean – without changing her. Are you – proposing tonight?"

Alexander set the box on his desktop. "No, I want to pick the right time and setting for it."

I looked away from Alexander and then looked back. "I still think that you should change her. I have recently been thinking about Kayal. If I had changed him he would still be alive today."

I hadn't heard my sister mention his name since he died. "Yes Antoinette, I remember but Ariel does not want to be changed either."

"You talked to her about it?"

"Yes I did. Antoinette you haven't mentioned Kayal in a very long time, are you alright?"

I quickly got hold of emotions. "Yes, and I am sorry that I mentioned him it was a long time ago." I turned around to leave.

"Wait a minute Antoinette. What aren't you telling me?"

I looked back at Alexander but didn't answer him. I walked out of the room. I knew deep down that Ariel was hiding something from Alexander and I also knew that it had to do with Luke but I just couldn't tell him.

* * *

After Antoinette left me I put my mother's ring box back into my desk drawer. I knew that Antoinette was upset but I didn't know why. I walked out of my office and down the staircase to the second floor then down the staircase to the first floor and down the hall to Ariel's door. I stopped and knocked. "Ariel, it is Alexander, are you still awake?"

"Come in."

I walked into Ariel's room. She was sitting in a chair by the fireplace reading. "What are you reading?"

"It is Shakespeare's greatest work, Romeo and Juliet."

I laughed. "I have read it myself, several times over." I walked over and stood next to her.

I looked up at Alexander. "Really Alexander I can't picture you reading this."

"Yes, I have read most of Shakespeare's works."

I smiled at him. "I guess that makes sense, I mean there wasn't television or much entertainment back then."

I laughed. "No there wasn't. I just came to tell you goodnight and that I love you."

"I love you too Alexander."

"I also want to remind you to be careful at school. Just because things have settled down doesn't mean that you aren't in any danger. We don't know where Luke or his friends are and he may come for you again."

"Oh Alexander, I don't think so." The look on Alexander's face told me that I had spoke too quickly.

"Ariel, why do you sound, so sure of that?"

I quickly composed myself. "I just mean that I don't think that Luke is interested in me. He stole Calicia's money and he is probably busy trying to start another coven somewhere."

"Yes, that is what Antoinette and I think too but that doesn't mean that he has forgotten about you."

"I don't care you will protect me?" It killed me to keep this secret from Alexander but I feared that if I told him that Luke had approached me at the pep rally that Alexander would hunt him to the ends of the earth. I couldn't go through another ordeal like what happened in Canada and risk loosing Alexander or Antoinette again.

"Ariel, you look tired."

"Yes, I am. I was just about finished reading anyway and was thinking about going to bed."

"Well then I will leave you. There is more work that I need to do in my office, good night."

Alexander bent over to kiss me and I tilted my head upward – we kissed and then parted. "Good night Alexander." After he left me I put my book down and got up from the chair and walked over to my bed and lay down. I thought about Antoinette and her mate Kayal whom Alexander had told me about and recalled that he said Antoinette blamed her self for his death. I wondered if that was the reason that she was so against Alexander and I being together. I thought about Luke and wondered where he was, I hoped that wherever he was that he was ok. Luke had protected me from Calicia Claig and I just couldn't forget that. Something in him had changed. I started to get sleepy and Alexander's face flashed back into my mind. I would be moving into the house permanently with Alexander and Antoinette. There was nothing in this world that I wanted more than Alexander. My eyes felt heavy.

* * *

I stood next to Ariel's bed side while she slept.

Her beautiful long red hair hung loosely around her face while her head rested on her pillow. I reached down and brushed a strand of it away from her face and she stirred slightly. I whispered softly, "Sleep my beautiful Ariel, I will be watching you and soon you will see that it is not Alexander that you love, it is me!"

My eyes opened abruptly and just for an instant I thought that I saw Luke standing next to my bed. I sat up in my bed and caught my breath and looked around the room, I was alone. I signed, "Oh, of all people to dream about," I told myself and then lay back down to go to sleep.

OTHER BOOKS BY R. STONE

(Reverse of the Curse Series)

Vampires 101

Vampires 200, Anatomy and Morphology of the Vampire, Part 1.

Vampires 201, Anatomy and Morphology of the Vampire, Part 2.

Vampires 202, The Immortals, coming soon.

(The Moon Watcher Series)

Sasquatch Moon, out in July 2014.

Half Moon of the Sasquatch, coming soon

Full Moon of the Sasquatch, coming soon

(Queen of Hearts Mini-Romance Series)

Sacred Hearts, coming soon.

The Embassy Connection, coming soon.

You can check these out at your favorite retailer.

Search: R. Stone Vampires
or R. Stone Sasquatch Moon

Also available in Kindle Version

AUTHOR BIOGRAPHY

The author, Shelly Stone started writing when she was a teenager and never really stopped. She lives with her dog Jake and three cats, Apollo, Pandora and Zena in South Dakota. She is part Chippewa Indian and has a great respect for nature. She writes a variety of books.

Visit with Shelly at themadwriter1.blog.com to see her other books.

www.ingramcontent.com/pod-product-compliance
Lightning Source LLC
Chambersburg PA
CBHW050947120626
46552CB00001B/426